ATOMIC REX

AFTERMATH OF ARMAGEDDON

MATTHEW DENNION

SEVERED PRESS
HOBART TASMANIA

ATOMIC REX

ISBN: 978-1-925342-47-5

In Loving Memory, of the filmmakers who created the wonderful Atomic Monster Films of the 1950' and 60's. Thanks for making my childhood a place of wonder and adventure!

To my Brother Mark, thanks for always challenging me and supporting me at the same time!

PROLOGUE

The morning sky was a dim orange as Chris Myers shifted the controls forward to move the fifty meter tall robot known as *Steel Samurai* onto the beach of Coney Island. The robot was an imposing figure that literally had the appearance of a giant samurai, including a helmet, and a twenty meter long sword. In addition to the sword, the robot was armed to the teeth with a giant crossbow, rockets, and high powered machine guns. Behind Steel Samurai were two more giant robots, known as *Iron Avenger*, and *Bronze Warrior*. Both of the robots were equally as well armed as Steel Samurai. The robots were piloted by Chris's best friend, Jeremy Draven, and Jeremy's girlfriend, Laura Swan. Together the three giant robots, or *mechs* as the media had dubbed them, represented humanity's best hope of preserving this last section of what was once the United States of America.

Chris was all too aware of the fact that the last hope which the mechs represented was a slim one. He seemed to recall an old song about living on a prayer, and as he stared at the Atlantic Ocean and the large swell of water approaching the beach, he wasn't even sure that humanity had a prayer.

Chris closed his eyes, and he thought about the events that had brought him to this point. He couldn't believe that in less than two years most of North America, and the rest of the world, had fallen under the control of the kaiju. It had all started with atomic tests taking place on a remote island in the Pacific Ocean. The world thought that the area tested on was only inhabited by sea birds and a few small mammals. The truth was that the governments of the world were all too eager to test their new weapons to check exactly what was on those islands. If someone had so much as flown over the island they would have noticed it was inhabited by a tribe of islanders and numerous prehistoric creatures.

Two months after the atomic bomb was detonated on the island, the first kaiju created by the blast attacked New Orleans. The monster was a huge turtle, nearly sixty meters long, whose saliva had been turned into a corrosive acid. The creature was given the name *Tortiraus*. There were reports that the monster was somehow able to fly and that it was seen splashing down in the Gulf of Mexico. Regardless of how Tortiraus arrived there, the kaiju quickly destroyed New Orleans. During his attack on the city, Tortiraus had proved nearly invulnerable to conventional weapons. The armed forces were simply unable to defeat the creature, and the entire Gulf of Mexico, as well as anything that was fifty kilometers inland from the Gulf, was declared Tortiraus's territory. The government decided that more lives would be saved by simply leaving the creature alone and moving away from it rather than attacking it again.

A week later a second creature had attacked San Francisco. This time the kaiju appeared to be one of the natives from the island that had been mutated into a monster. The islander was now a fifty-five meter tall giant with a huge bloated gut. When the giant entered the city he began devouring everything thing that he encountered. The kaiju devoured any meat that he could find. Fish, horses, cows, dogs, even people were grabbed up by the giant and tossed into his mouth. Some idiot blogger had named the giant *Yokozuna*. Apparently the name means something like *grand sumo champion* in Japanese. Whatever the name meant it quickly stuck to the giant, and he was officially designated as Yokozuna. When it became clear that the armed forces were unable to defeat the creature, everything from Northern California to Canada was declared Yokozuna's territory, and everyone who was still alive in the area was evacuated.

After Yokozuna, more reports started to come in from all over the world. Sightings of monsters in the oceans, and then reports of attacks on other countries began appearing up all over the internet. To further complicate matters, the radiation given off by Tortiraus and Yokozuna spread like a plague and created other giant mutations. For the most part, these mutations were lesser kaiju, like giant bugs or rodents. While the Army was able to destroy these creatures individually, the sheer number of giant mutants quickly became a problem.

A group of giant ants dubbed the Colony had been mutated by Yokozuna. The Colony moved into Los Angeles where they also began devouring people. Once again humans were forced to evacuate and give L.A. to the monsters.

In response to the growing crisis, The U.S. government quickly approved a plan to create their own atomic monsters in the form of giant nuclear powered robots. A dozen robots were created to retake The Northern West Coast and the Gulf of Mexico. For the first time since Tortiraus had gained control of the South Eastern United States, the people of the world had hope. That hope lasted until the first robot, Steel Sentry, challenged Tortiraus and the kaiju tore through Steel Sentry as if it were made of aluminum foil. The same thing happened when another of the mechs challenged Yokozuna. After only two battles, the number of mechs had been reduced to ten while the number of kaiju continued to increase.

Giladon, a quadrupedal monster that resembled a colossal Gila monster, came ashore next in the Sea of Cortez. The monster made its way up into Utah, Wyoming, and Colorado where it killed millions of people. This time two mechs went to challenge the beast, but Giladon destroyed them both.

Giladon had no sooner claimed his territory than a twenty foot tall creature, that looked a like a heavily muscled man with pitch black skin and long fangs, suddenly showed up in New Mexico and Arizona. No one seemed to know where the monster had come from. It literally just fell out of the sky one day right into the middle of Santa Fe. The creature was dubbed *Ogre* by those that survived the beast's attack on Santa Fe. Ogre was small by the standards of the other monsters that had appeared as he was only about six meters tall. Several theories began to spring up about what exactly Ogre had formerly been. One theory was that Ogre was a primate who had lived on the island and was turned into a monster from the atomic tests conducted there. Other people speculated that the he was at one time a human who had been mutated by Giladon when the kaiju had made his way through the Southwest.

Whatever Ogre was, despite his smaller size, he was perhaps the most physically powerful and destructive atomic monster that had yet to appear. The creature was able to smash a skyscraper to the ground with a single blow. His legs were powerful enough that when he jumped into the air that a single leap carried him several miles at a time. Once more, two mechs were sent into battle Ogre, and the mutant turned them both into scrap metal. There were a few vague reports that Ogre had grabbed a couple of young women and jumped off with them. With the carnage that had occurred in Santa Fe, there was no way to confirm these reports. If anyone was taken by the monster they were officially presumed dead.

Two more kaiju appeared from the island shortly after Ogre. The first creature went totally unnoticed as it slid off the island and made its way into Mexico. The kaiju was an ameba that had grown to an immense size. The creature was given the name *Amebos* when it came ashore in Mexico and quickly began absorbing anything and everything that it crawled over. The fact that the creature had no body structure made it difficult to attack. The U.S. decided that mechs would not even be sent in to try and contend with Amebos. Like so many other vast areas of land, the entire country of Mexico was simply left to the monster.

A month after Amebos had taken over Mexico, the next attack occurred. This time a semi-aquatic mutated bipedal dinosaur with two large sails on his back left the island before the U.S. Navy was able to set up a blockade around it. The creature swam north and landed in Alaska. The kaiju was given the name *Dimetrasaurs* because of its similarity in appearance to the dinosaur known as dimetrodon. One of the remaining mechs met Dimetrasaurs as it was preparing to cross the Canadian border. There was an extended battle, but once more, the kaiju prevailed over the mech.

Dimetrasaurs cleared a path across Canada prior to making its way into the Great Lakes. The government sent the mech known as *Metal Master* to stop the creature from entering U.S. territory, and once more, the monster was successful in defeating the mech. The last that was heard of Metal Master, both the mech, and his pilot, were sinking to the bottom of Lake Michigan with Dimetrasaurs clamped onto them. The kaiju had won the Great Lakes. It moved freely between them, and all of the towns and cities which bordered the Lakes had to be evacuated. Anyone living between Minnesota and Northwest Pennsylvania had to be moved out of their homes.

All of the evacuated people had made their way to the now extremely over crowded North East United States. Steel Samurai, Iron Avenger, and Bronze Warrior had cleared out a nest of gigantic spiders that had gathered in the area, and it looked like the area would be safe for humans. The more powerful kaiju had established their territories, the Naval blockade was finally set up around the island, and it included the two remaining mechs outside of the North East.

Back home Chris and his friends had proven that with their mechs they could handle the lesser giant mutants that might attack the Northeast. With the Northeast secure, the government was addressing how to get what aid that they could to the displaced citizens when the news had come from the island that a new kaiju was trying to escape.

The kaiju was a T-Rex like creature, except that its arms were exceptionally long and powerful. The length and build of the creature's arms looked more proportional to a human than they did to a dinosaur. The beast had a hard serrated caprice on his back like that of an alligator or crocodile. The creature walked in the same manner as a T-Rex with its legs underneath it, and its thick tail acting as a counter balance to the rest of its body. The kaiju had a height of roughly fifty meters at the shoulder blade and a length of nearly sixty-five meters.

The creature's appearance was terrifying, but its strength and power were awe inspiring. When it was first sighted heading for the beach one of the two mechs guarding the island flew directly for the creature and attacked it. The mech delivered a blow that would have turned a skyscraper into rubble, but the monster just absorbed the blow as if it were nothing more than a gentle breeze. The creature quickly retaliated by clamping its jaws onto the torso of the mech and using its long arms to grab the robot's legs. In one swift motion, the kaiju tore the mech in half.

The remaining mech and the ships of the Naval blockade didn't waste time seeing what the monster's next move would be. They opened fire with everything they had on the beast. Four warships and a giant mech unleashed their fury on the kaiju, and in the process, turned the beach into a hell on Earth. Shells and gunfire engulfed the creature in flames and smoke. The smoke had still yet to clear when a roar came out of the darkness. The roar was followed by a wave of sheer atomic radiation that destroyed all four warships and the mech in a single attack. Only a few of the crew members of the ship farthest from the beach survived for brief time before dying from radiation poisoning. When a rescue ship had picked up the crew they asked them *what kind of monster had escaped from the island?* The crew members looked at each for a moment, and then, one said the words, *"Atomic Rex!"*

The monster swam through the Pacific, and then he crossed Central America by making landfall near the Panama Canal. The creature then entered the Atlantic Ocean where it made its way north. Atomic Rex moved at an incredible speed, but the military noticed that he gave a wide berth to the Gulf of Mexico. There was speculation that Atomic Rex could sense Tortiraus and that he did not want to engage the acid spewing giant turtle. After it swam up the Gulf Stream, Atomic Rex took a sharp turn and headed for New York City.

Chris opened his eyes to find his forehead covered in sweat as he recalled the events that had brought him to this point. He looked out at the ocean again to see the saurian head of Atomic Rex rising out of the water. He thought to himself that if four warships and two mechs were unable to stop the creature, then what chance did three mechs have?

As if in answer to Chris's question, Jeremy's voice came over the radio, "Two more refugee trains have headed for Kansas, but there are still several million people in the Tri-State area alone that need our protection." Jeremy was silent for a moment, "Remember we are going to try and buy them as much time as we can to get out of here, but one of us needs to leave this battle with our mech intact. It will be up to that person to defend the settlement from any future kaiju attacks. Are you both clear on that?"

Laura responded with a grim determination in her voice, "Yes baby, I got it."

Chris stammered, "I…I got it too, buddy."

Jeremy tried to sound enthusiastic as he replied, "Okay then, let's give this reject from a B-movie something to think about before he comes ashore."

All three mechs stood side by side and fired every projectile weapon they had at once at the oncoming kaiju. A breathtaking cascade of water and fire shrouded the kaiju as the mechs fired upon the beast.

As it did on the beach of the island, Atomic Rex roared in defiance, and then retaliated with his radioactive abilities. When Chris had heard about the monster's Atomic Wave attack he had pictured it like a wave on the ocean coming out of the monster's body, but it was so much more than that. Chris gasped as a massive translucent dome emanated out from Atomic Rex. The dome was several hundred feet high and quickly expanded. The closest thing Chris could compare it to was when the warriors on those old anime movies were showing off their power as they upped their chi.

The dome shot across the ocean, and when it hit the beach, Chris saw the reeds on the sand dunes wither and die instantly. Before the mechs could move, the dome struck them with the force of a hurricane. All three mechs were sent hurtling backward. Chris's entire body was jarred when Steel Samurai hit the ground. His ears were still ringing when he heard Jeremy's voice come through the radio.

"Chris, fall back to the rallying point! We are going to cover your escape."

Chris had thought that Laura and Jeremy already had their mechs up and were attacking Atomic Rex, but when he got Steel Samurai to its feet, he saw that his friends were still trying to get their robots off the ground. That's when it dawned on him that the future of the human race had fallen squarely on his shoulders. Laura and Jeremy were in love. There was no way that one of them wanted to go on without the other. As soon as they had been directed to engage Atomic Rex they had decided that they would go down together.

Iron Avenger and Bronze Warrior lifted themselves off the ground and together they charged the most powerful creature that had ever walked the face of the Earth. Chris watched in stunned silence as he heard their conversation over his radio.

"I love you, Jeremy! I will see you on the other side!"

Jeremy sobbed as he replied, "I love you too, Laura."

The two mechs jumped at Atomic Rex, and they began reigning down blows on the monster. The kaiju was momentarily staggered by the fury of their attack. Atomic Rex actually fell to one knee as the mechs assaulted him.

For the briefest moment, Chris thought that his friends would be okay. He thought that they would be able to defeat the monster. He thought that he might not be left as the lone protector of humanity, and then reality came crashing down in the form of an enraged mutated dinosaur.

Atomic Rex shot up from the ground and closed his jaws on the top half of Bronze Warrior. With the robot in his grasp, he crushed the mech like a ripe grape, ending Laura's life instantly.

Iron Avenger went into a frenzy as Jeremy channeled his rage into the robot. Iron Avenger's arms were a blur as it pounded on Atomic Rex, but the monster was not affected by Jeremy's anger or the robot's blows. With a single swipe of his arm, Atomic Rex knocked Iron Avenger's left arm and shoulder off. A swipe from the kaiju's other arm separated Iron Avenger's torso from his legs.

Jeremy crawled out of the wreckage of his mech, and he immediately fell to his knees. He moaned in pain and began vomiting due to the radiation pouring off of the monster. Chris watched for two agonizing minutes as his friend's body blistered and bled before finally giving out.

Atomic Rex didn't even notice Jeremy next to his foot. The monster was staring at Steel Samurai and waiting for the metallic centurion to attack. When Jeremy died Chris came to his senses. He hit the ignition button and sent Steel Samurai shooting up into the air.

As Atomic Rex watched the last challenge to his domain flee the kaiju threw his head back and roared in triumph. The monster then lowered his head and glared at the city that represented his new kingdom!

CHAPTER 1

Three Years later.
Kansas

Chris woke and stared at the wall of his shack before climbing out of bed. He smelled himself and then winced at the odor of dried sweat that wafted off his clothes. He knew he should wander down to the freshwater stream at the back of the settlement and wash himself off, but he guessed that a lot of people would be down at the stream either bathing or boiling water. If he went down to the stream, though, he'd get stares of disgust and then the under the breath comments would start about: *Good for nothing coward,* and, *Should give that mech over to someone who knows what he is doing.*

Chris opted to wait in his cabin until nightfall, and then sneak off to get a bath. He was stretching out when he heard someone outside of his cabin shout, "Thanks a hell of a lot for letting those bugs eat up all of the wheat! I guess that we can eat cake this winter because there sure as hell won't be any bread. Maybe next time you can fire a rocket or two at the damn things."

Anger coursed through Chris as he threw open the door to his cabin in search of the man who had yelled at him. He looked for the heckler, but whoever had made the comments had already faded back into the thousands of tents that comprised what was left of the United States of America. Chris shook his head and then closed the door to his cabin. He slammed his fist into the door and cursed, "God Dammit! If they think that they can do the job better then let them do it. It's not like I asked for this job." He paced back and forth across his small cabin. "Sure, I'll just use some rockets on the things. That way not only would I use up some of the limited supply of heavy weapons that I have but I would have blown up even more of the crops."

Chris leaned against the wall of his cabin, and then slid down it crying as he thought about how his life had changed since the Dawn of the Kaiju. After Atomic Rex had claimed New York and the rest of the Northeast as his territory, hundreds of thousands of people had migrated to Kanas where they set up a massive tent city. In addition to the ragged tents, the settlement had a few cabins for the leaders, doctors, and other key figures. Since he was the pilot of Steel Samurai, Chris was also given a cabin.

The first winter in the settlement was tough. The city lost about twenty-five percent of its population to the bitter cold. Thousands of people had literally frozen to death as they slept. The next year saw a flu sweep through the city, and given the conditions that they lived in and the lack of medical supplies, the flu killed another fifteen percent of the population.

There was also the occasional lower threat nomadic monster like a giant shrew or rabbit. When the monsters would attack they would always manage to kill a few people before Chris could activate Steel Samurai and fight off the mutant. All in all, over three hundred thousand people had dropped to less than seventy-five thousand people in less than three years. The people relied on the vast wheat fields of Kansas to provide bread, which was the main staple of their diet. The fact that the settlement relied so heavily on the grain is what made yesterday's attack so devastating. Chris could still see the sky turning black as the sun was blocked out by hundreds of twenty meter tall grasshoppers. The mutants flew directly over the settlement, and then they descended on the wheat fields. Chris got into Steel Samurai as quickly as he could and headed for the field.

The mech began slicing through giant grasshoppers like they were paper, but there were just too many of them. The grasshoppers didn't try to fight or run, they just keep eating even as Chris was cutting them in half. By the time that Steel Samurai had killed the last bug more than fifty percent of the crop was gone. With that kind of hit, the settlement would be facing starvation. The old, the sick, the very young, and even some of the young and healthy people would die a slow and hungry death.

Only a few months after he had arrived at the settlement, Chris could see that it wouldn't last long. He knew that between limited resources, climate, and kaiju that the settlement was a last stand for humanity and not the new beginning that the settlement leaders spoke of it as. It was this view that had kept Chris from falling in love and starting a family. When he had first arrived his status as Steel Samurai's pilot gave him sort of a rock star status. Women threw themselves at him. He was not beyond a one night stand, but with a lack of birth control methods, there was always the chance that he could get a girl pregnant. It was not the thought of being a father that bothered Chris, in fact he had always wanted to be a father, but not in these circumstances. How could he bring a child into the world when he knew that the kid's life would be short and full of pain, hunger, cold, and fear?

Chris was still wallowing in his own depression when there was a frantic knocking on his door. Chris yelled, "Go away! I did all that I could yesterday. Without me and Steel Samurai, there wouldn't be any crops left at all."

Chris started to walk back to bed when the knocking started again.

"Captain Myers, there are kaiju coming out of the stream!"

A look of shock came across Chris's face as he cursed to himself. He stood there silently for a second as he processed what the implications of a kaiju in the stream meant. When the voice outside screamed his name again, he snapped back into action and ran out of his cabin.

He knocked over the man who had been banging on the door and ran to the gargantuan form of Steel Samurai. The mech stood like a silent sentry on the outskirts of the tent settlement roughly five hundred meters from Chris's cabin. It took Chris two minutes at a full sprint to reach the giant robot and another minute to scale the thing and climb inside the cockpit.

Chris turned the mech on, hit the ignition, and sent Steel Samurai shooting into the air and over the settlement. The stream was about a kilometer away from the far side of the city from where the mech was stationed. Steel Samurai could make the distance in a matter of seconds without even coming close to top speed.

Chris immediately saw people fleeing from the stream, and he could also see three blood red large flat forms in the middle of the water. Chris muttered to himself, "Great, giant mutated leeches." Chris watched as one of the leeches slithered out of the stream and right on top of several fleeing people. He could not see under the monster's body, but he was sure that there were people trapped in the kaiju's mouth where it was draining the blood from their bodies. Since the monsters were attacking from the stream that served as the water source for everyone, Chris had to be careful about how he handled the situation. He had Steel Samurai fly over the leech that was feeding. He knew that while the monster was feeding it would remain still for a while. He also knew that there was nothing that he could do for the people being exsanguinated in the monster's mouth.

Steel Samurai grabbed one of the two leeches still in the stream in each of its hands. The robot lifted them out of the water and flew about a kilometer away from the stream before it dropped them onto the ground. The mech landed in front of them as the two monsters lifted their bodies off the ground so that Chris was looking directly into the creatures' horrible mouths. For a brief moment, Chris shuddered as he thought about the people who were still dying in the third leech's mouth.

The two leeches in front of Chris lashed out as they tried to attach their mouths to Steel Samurai. The leeches' mouths slid harmlessly off of the mech's body as Chris had the robot pull back his sword, and then slice the two beasts in half. Four sections of giant leech writhed on the ground in front of Steel Samurai as Chris tried to remember if leeches could regenerate or not. What he did know was that slicing up to two leeches to have them come back as four leeches would not be a smart move. Figuring that it was better to be safe than sorry Chris had Steel Samurai point his arm at the creatures, and he used his flamethrower to burn the monsters to cinders.

Steel Samurai took the sky and flew back over the stream just as the last remaining leech started to slither toward the settlement. The mech landed behind the beast, and then once more Chris used its flamethrower to burn the monster to death.

Chris was still sitting in the cockpit of Steel Samurai as he considered the most important question about the leeches' appearance in the stream. If the leeches were mutated when they crawled into the stream then they were a minor threat that Steel Samurai could easily deal with. The other possibility was a death sentence for the settlement. If the leeches were turned into giants because the stream was contaminated by radiation then the water supply for the last known settlement of humans in North America was now poison.

CHAPTER 2

The settlement had a meeting that night as the leaders tried to address the concerns of the population. The weather was hot and humid. The crushing heat meant that the people's already volatile attitudes would be inflamed even further.

Chris stood off to the side of the makeshift stage where the settlement leaders were positioned. An angry man moved up to the front of the stage and began screaming at the leaders, "First our food supply is damaged, and now there are monsters in the water! Is it safe to eat wheat from the fields and use the water?"

One of the leaders stood. "What remains of the wheat crop is safe. Captain Myers was careful to eliminate the grasshoppers as surgically as possible. Any strains of wheat that had irradiated blood fall onto it has been removed. With proper rationing, we believe that we will have enough bread to get us through the next year. Hopefully by that time the crops will have regrown completely."

The leader paused for a moment. "We do not know about the water supply yet. We are testing the water on several different flora and fauna. If they do not show any adverse effects then the water is safe. Until we know for sure if the water is safe or not, the stream will be quarantined."

The crowd grumbled and another man started shouting, "What do we do if the water is contaminated? What do we do if another swarm of giant bugs attacks what remains of the crops? What are you people doing to keep us from starving or dying of dehydration?"

A roar of shouts followed the man's rant as another of the settlement leaders tried to reassure everyone that plans were being put in to place to deal with either of those two scenarios should they come to fruition.

The crowd was still shouting as Chris walked away from the meeting. He had spoken with the town elders earlier that day and had informed them that either way if the water was irradiated or not the settlement could only last another two years at most.

Two attacks in less than twenty-four hours and a slowly increasing frequency of attacks prior to that was a clear indication that things were only to get worse. The True Kaiju: Atomic Rex, Tortiraus, Amebos, Ogre, The Colony, Giladon, Yokozuna, and Dimetrasaurs all controlled the most vital areas of the country. With increased attacks from lesser mutated monsters like the giant grasshoppers and leeches, it meant that radiation from the True Kaiju was creating more and more mutants by the day. To further compound matters, the True Kaiju were all known to be highly territorial. If another kaiju showed up in their territory they would either kill the creature or drive it away. So as the ambient radiation from the True Kaiju created more mutants these creatures were forced to leave the area where they were spawned in order to avoid being killed by their more powerful creators. Thus the only option left to these lesser beasts was to move to the area of the middle of the country where the settlement was currently located. Once they arrived these lesser monsters would then sustain themselves on the humans or their supplies. It was a vicious cycle that would quickly lead to humanity's demise.

Chris had almost reached his cabin when he saw the monolithic but nearly useless form of Steel Samurai in front of him. The so called *mighty robot* was nothing but a life support system for the dying race known as humanity. As long as the True Kaiju existed the lesser monsters would keep coming. With his mech, Chris could continue to fight them off, but the settlement would lose food, people, and water in each battle. Chris wondered if he should stop fighting altogether. He began to think that the people around him would be spared a good deal of pain and suffering if he were to just let the monsters take them all out in the next attack. After all, as long as the True Kaiju existed they would continue to spawn more mutants, and there was no way in hell that Steel Samurai could kill the True Kaiju because there was no force on Earth that could defeat those beasts.

As that thought crossed Chris's mind another thought quickly followed it. He stared at Steel Samurai, and then he voiced the thought aloud as if doing so would bring more validity to it, "The one thing that might be able to defeat one of the True Kaiju is another True Kaiju." Chris began to walk toward Steel Samurai at a faster pace as he continued to verbalize his plan to himself, "The kaiju are highly territorial and aggressive. I could use Steel Samurai to attack the kaiju one by one. I don't have to beat them, I just need to last long enough and keep them engaged enough to follow me into another creature's territory. The other monster will sense the threat to its domain and attack the invader. When the second kaiju appears on my radar I can take off and let the two monsters battle to the death. One of them will kill the other, and if I'm really lucky, two creatures will be killed in the battle."

Chris ran into his cabin and began throwing whatever food and water that he had into a sack. Once he had enough provisions to last him for a few weeks he crept back out into the settlement. As soon as he exited his cabin he could hear the shouts from the settlement meeting. For a brief second, Chris thought that maybe leaving these people totally unprotected was the wrong thing to do. Then Chris thought to himself that being a protector was not the answer. These people were beyond needing a protector. They needed a savior, and the only way that Chris could hope to become that savior was to enact his plan. If he enacted his plan nearly everyone in the settlement would see him as quitting and leaving them to die at the hands of monsters. He hoped that one day if he was successful that someone would figure out what he did and that he would not be remembered as a deserter and a coward. The bright side was that if he was a failure that it wouldn't matter what the people of the settlement thought of him because they would all be dead very soon.

Chris shrugged, and then he began climbing Steel Samurai. When he entered the robot he brought up a display of where the True Kaiju were all located. He also brought up a description of each kaiju's strength and weakness. It quickly became clear to him that Tortiraus and Atomic Rex seemed to be the two most powerful creatures. If that was the case then they would be two of his *cleaners*. They would be the monsters that he used to terminate the other True Kaiju. Once every other creature was destroyed then he would have Tortiraus and Atomic Rex meet and battle. Chris briefly thought it strange that the two most powerful creatures would have territories next to each other, and then he thought that maybe the kaiju super powers had set it up that way so that they could have an eye on their potential rival. Either way, Chris decided that the monsters out west had a much more even playing field, and he decided to start thinning out the herd there. He also figured that he would have the better chance of surviving an encounter with some of those creatures than he would against Atomic Rex or Tortiraus. With that in mind, Chris started up Steel Samurai's ignition, and the mighty robot shot up into the sky.

The leaders were still trying to calm the people of the settlement, but when they saw Steel Samurai fly across the night sky and out of sight, the concerned settlers quickly became a scared mob. With their protection gone, the people of the settlement went into a panic.

CHAPTER 3

Egg Harbor, New Jersey

The very ground shook with each step that the mighty kaiju took as he strode across his domain. Every time that his powerful foot came crashing to the ground rodents scurried into their burrows and birds took off into the air. Atomic Rex was moving across the highway that was once the Garden State Parkway at a rapid pace. Atomic Rex was the king of his domain and typically there was no reason for him to be in a hurry to get anywhere. The kaiju simply lumbered across his land at a comfortable pace until he reached his destination.

Today, however, the monster moved with a definite purpose in mind. Atomic Rex was not simply wandering across his domain. The monster was moving to attack an invader to his territory. The kaiju did not understand the sensation that was driving him to Egg Harbor. The beast simply knew that his senses told him that another kaiju had come to his land. While the beast did not know what the structure was, he did comprehend that the nuclear power plant in Egg Harbor was one of his primary sources of sustenance. Atomic Rex knew that when he felt tired or low on energy that he could go to the funnel shaped structure and that it would reinvigorate him. Now there was another beast that was not only in his territory but it was also feeding off of the radiation from the power plant. This invader was literally stealing Atomic Rex's power source.

Atomic Rex stepped off the Parkway and began cutting through the woods in a direct path to the power plant. A few minutes later Atomic Rex was able to see the large funnel that constituted the Egg Harbor Nuclear Power Plant.

The kaiju stepped into the shallow water of the wetlands that surrounded the plant. The monster stood motionless for a moment as his senses took in the area. Atomic Rex's eyes could see for several kilometers. He also possessed the greatest sense of smell in the world. The mutated dinosaur could smell everything within fifty kilometers of his position. Like the sharks in the ocean, Atomic Rex's mutated body could sense the miniscule electrical pulses given off by the organisms living around him. The kaiju could tell if a mouse was burrowing into the ground within fifty meters of him. Even with his enhanced senses, Atomic Rex was unable to detect a single living creature anywhere near the power plant. Despite the lack of evidence, Atomic Rex instinctively knew that there was another kaiju close by.

Atomic Rex bent down low to the wetlands around his feet and unleashed a deafening roar that echoed across the empty landscape. As the roar shot across the wetlands the surface of the water began to move. The water moved in conjunction with the roar in the direction of the power plant. Long after the force from the roar had dissipated, the water continued to move in the direction of the power plant. As the water moved it gained momentum. Soon not just the water, but reeds, seaweed, mud, logs, algae and everything else that composed the wetland estuary began to move toward the power plant. The moving landscape began to pile up on top of itself at the base of the power plant.

Atomic Rex watched as the quickly building mound of muck and plants began to form arms, legs, hands, and even a kind of head. After the body of the creature had formed, multiple yellow colored flowers began to converge in the center of the face. The flowers created two large orbs that looked like glowing yellow eyes. When the creature was fully formed it stared at Atomic Rex and stretched its arms out in front of the power plant. Atomic Rex watched as droplets fell off of the monster's arms and onto the concrete of the power plant. Every drop from the monster's body burned directly through the three feet thick concrete walls of the power plant.

When the droplets hit the power plant, Atomic Rex was finally able to smell the acid that dripped off of the creature. To the humans the plant creature was known as *Marsh-Thing*. While the creature's body was composed of plants and muck, it was actually trillions and trillions of microbes that gave the beast life. Shortly after Tortiraus had taken over the Gulf of Mexico, the acid spewing kaiju turtle took up residence in the Florida Everglades for several weeks. The beast's ambient radiation and acid caused many of the flora and fauna in the Everglades to mutate into giant monsters and other horrors. Giant alligators and pythons were some of the first mutants that Tortiraus had inadvertently spawned. The turtle monster killed most of these giants, but a few members of each species had made their way out to sea or farther north into Atomic Rex's domain.

It was not until Tortiraus had left that the microbes his body had mutated started to crave the radiation the kaiju gave off. The microbes searched throughout the Everglades for additional forms of radiation. They fed off of lesser mutants and radioactive waste. Once they had exhausted the Everglades of radiation the microbes realized they needed to leave the swamp in order to locate more radioactive substances. The microbes were faced with the problem of not being able to leave the swamp, while at the same time, feeling an insatiable drive to absorb radiation. The microbes solved the problem by forcing the swamp to come with them as they went in search of radiation. The microbes attached their bodies to various aspects of the swamp, and then they forced those pieces together into the walking heap of swamp that was Marsh-Thing. The plants and mud of the Everglades were soaked in the acid that Tortiraus had left behind. When the microbes had meshed the contents of the swamp into a single walking nightmare the highly acidic content of the materials that composed it gave Marsh- Thing an acidic touch. Anything thing that came into contact with the creature would be subjected to a touch that burned with the fury of sulfuric acid.

Marsh-Thing made its way up the coast absorbing whatever radiation that it could find until it stumbled upon the Egg Harbor Nuclear Power Plant. The microbes that constituted Marsh-Thing did not have the same level of intelligence as some of the other kaiju. The monster had no idea that he had entered into Atomic Rex's territory or that it was draining radiation from one of Atomic Rex's most frequented power sources.

As Marsh-Thing was holding on to the power plant the countless microbes that held the creature together sensed the awesome power emanating from Atomic Rex. Marsh-Thing slid off of the side of the power plant, and then it began to take slow, plodding steps toward Atomic Rex.

Atomic Rex was already furious that this strange beast had invaded his territory and had been draining his power source, but when he saw the mountain of muck advancing toward him to attack, he went into a rage. Atomic Rex roared and charged at Marsh-Thing. The two kaiju met in the middle of the vast wetland that surrounded the power plant. They slammed into each other with the force of two tectonic plates colliding deep within the bowels of the Earth.

Atomic Rex was the stronger of the two kaiju, and he pushed Marsh-Thing backward as he wrapped his arms around the muck monster and bit into its shoulder. Atomic Rex immediately released both his grip and his bite as the acid from Marsh-Thing's body burned into the mutated dinosaur's mouth and skin. Atomic Rex shook his head from side to side as he attempted to remove the painful acid from his mouth.

With his opponent backing away from him, Marsh-Thing stepped forward and pressed his attack. The swamp monster grabbed the dinosaur by the neck, and as Atomic Rex roared in pain from his acidic touch, Marsh-Thing stared at the nuclear powered creature. The microbes composing Marsh-Thing felt the energy emanating out of Atomic Rex. Atomic Rex shook his powerful head from side to side and he not only broke Marsh-Thing's grip, but he sent the muck monster's entire right arm flying out into the wetlands.

Atomic Rex roared at the slime covered kaiju. Then, the nuclear dinosaur quickly grabbed Marsh-Thing, and despite the sensation of acid burning through his skin, Atomic Rex threw Marsh-Thing to the ground. When Marsh-Thing hit the ground its soft body splattered into thousands of pieces. Atomic Rex lifted his head into the air and roared in triumph. The monster was about to walk over to the prize of the power plant when he saw the water in front of him beginning to pile on top of itself.

A second later the reformed Marsh-Thing rose out of the wetlands and wrapped its acid filled arms around Atomic Rex. Atomic Rex fought desperately to free himself from the painful grip of Marsh-Thing, but the living swamp refused to release his grip.

Ignoring the searing pain assaulting his torso, Atomic Rex grabbed a hold of Marsh-Thing. The mutated dinosaur then lifted Marsh-Thing off his feet, and he slammed his opponent into the ground. Marsh-Thing attempted to stand when Atomic Rex brought his clawed foot crashing down into the mound of mud that was Marsh-Thing. Atomic Rex pulled his burning foot out of Marsh-Thing, and then brought it down onto the monster again. Atomic Rex repeated the move several times before he had finally stomped Marsh-Thing's body into the watery wetlands.

Atomic Rex was intelligent enough to comprehend that Marsh-Thing had come back once before when he had thought the swamp creature to have been vanquished. Atomic Rex strained his enhanced senses to the limit looking for any sign that Marsh-Thing was attempting to reconstitute itself for another attack. It was in the dinosaur's still burning feet that he felt Marsh-Thing moving to attack him again. Atomic Rex could feel the wet mud that his feet were buried in pressing up against him. An instant later, the floor of the very wetlands themselves shot up Atomic Rex's body and completely covered him. Every nerve in Atomic Rex's body was screaming in pain as the acidic contents of Marsh-Thing burned his skin. A moment later, the wet mud that was Marsh-Thing worked its way into Atomic Rex's nose, ears, and mouth, burning the interior of his body, as well as his skin. Atomic Rex was enduring a level of pain that he had never experienced before. Even the bright flash that had changed him from the Tyrannosaur that he had previously been into the kaiju that he currently was, did not cause as much pain as the Marsh-Thing enveloping him.

Atomic Rex fell to the ground and rolled from side to side through the saltwater of the wetlands in an attempt to free himself from the excruciating attack, but the Marsh-Thing was unrelenting. Atomic Rex was beginning to blackout when his indomitable will to survive kicked in. The kaiju forced his body back to his feet, and then he reached deep within himself to the nuclear energy that powered every single one of his cells. Atomic Rex focused on that power, and then he sent it cascading out of his body in the form of his Atomic Wave. The mud and plants that the microbes which composed Marsh-Thing were attached to were sent hurtling away from Atomic Rex riding the kaiju's Atomic Wave blast. As the nuclear dome forced the microbes off of Atomic Rex's body they also filled the power hungry microbes with more atomic energy than their microscopic forms could hold. One by one trillions of microbes burst from the sheer energy that they had attempted to absorb.

Mere seconds after Atomic Rex had unleashed his Atomic Wave attack, the battle was over. The microbes that were Marsh-Thing had been completely destroyed. Just as Atomic Rex sensed that there was an incursion into his domain he could also sense that the threat posed by the invader was no more. This time Atomic Rex was sure that he had finally destroyed his enemy. The kaiju once more lifted his head into the air, and then he unleashed a deafening roar that proclaimed to the world that he had defended his territory.

When Atomic Rex lowered his head he felt the radiation from the nuclear power plant calling to him. The kaiju's Atomic Wave attack had cracked the exterior of the nuclear reactor, and now its energy was pouring out of the concrete monolith like it had never done before. Atomic Rex walked almost reverently over to the reactor where he soaked up the spoils of his victory.

CHAPTER 4

Santa Fe, New Mexico

The interior of the empty warehouse was hot, and the smell from the bloated and rotting bodies stuffed inside it was nearly unbearable. Of the nine women who had been brought to the warehouse two years ago only three of them survived. The monster known as Ogre had captured the women and taken them back to the warehouse that served as his den. The women were not sure why Ogre had brought them there. They had assumed that Ogre had captured them in order to eat them. They were surprised when instead of eating them, Ogre actually brought them food. The food was presented in the form of raw meat from either cattle or wild bison. The interesting aspect of the food was that it was unaffected by radiation. It seemed as if Ogre had realized that the women required food that was radiation free in order to survive. When Ogre brought them food the women began to realize that their fates were not to be eaten but rather to be Ogre's companions.

The six meter tall Ogre rarely interacted with the women in any way other than simply sitting by them and watching them. The women would talk amongst themselves and one of the things that came up was the rumor that Ogre may have once been a man who was turned into a monster by radiation. They began to speculate that if Ogre had once been a man then perhaps he felt some need to have other humans around him. The women further surmised that they were being held prisoner by Ogre in order to meet his need for having other people around. They further speculated that if Ogre had been a man who was mutated by radiation that it would explain why he was careful to only bring the women food that was uncontaminated by radiation.

The warehouse was also one of the few buildings left standing that had running water. Luckily the water supply for Santa Fe had thus far been uncontaminated. The choice of the warehouse, his ability to detect radiation, and his realization that it would kill his captives all seemed to lend credence to the idea that Ogre had some level of intelligence.

When the women realized the role they were serving for Ogre they also realized that they would be spending the rest of their lives in the warehouse. This caused a panic to run through them. None of them wanted to spend the rest of their lives as a prisoner to a horrifying beast.

Cassie Singleton was the first to try and escape from the warehouse. She had no sooner run across the parking light than the dark form of Ogre came falling out of the sky. The monster roared at Cassie before crushing her to a pulp with a single blow. The monster seemed angry that one of his possessions would attempt to flee from him. Ogre stepped on the bloody remains of Cassie and rubbed his foot in her entrails as he was looking back to the warehouse at the other women who were watching him. It almost seemed as if the monster was sending a message to the other women that any further attempts to escape would be met with the same punishment.

Two months had passed before Erin Kennedy attempted to make a run for it. She put a good deal more planning in to her escape than Cassie had. Erin studied Ogre's habits and took note of how often he would leave the warehouse, and how long he would be gone each time that he was out. She realized that when Ogre went out to hunt he was often gone for at least two hours before returning with beef for both himself and the captive women to share. Erin had explained her plan to the remaining eight women, and two more of them decided to join her in her attempt to run to freedom.

They waited twenty minutes until after Ogre had left, and then they made a break for it. The five women who had stayed behind watched from one of the warehouse windows as their fellow captives attempted to flee from the living nightmare that they were trapped in. They watched as Erin and her two followers sprinted across the parking lot. The spectators cheered when Erin reached the fence to the warehouse and climbed over it, with her friends following closely behind her. Erin waved the other two girls on as she was running down the middle of the street and away from Ogre's warehouse. They had made it several blocks when the girls watching from the warehouse saw a large black shape moving toward them from overhead.

The group watching from the warehouse screamed in terror as they thought that the shape was Ogre, but then they noticed that the shape was flying in a straight line and not moving in an arching leap like Ogre did. Not only was the flight pattern different, but as the shape moved in on Erin, the women in the warehouse could see that the shape was far larger than Ogre. Erin screamed in terror as the shadow of the creature fell upon her and her friends. The giant wasp was roughly forty meters long, and when it landed in front of Erin and the other two women, it totally blocked the street.

The three woman turned around and tried to run away, but the giant wasp was far quicker than the women were. The wasp reached down and bit Erin in half with one chomp of its massive mandibles. Erin's legs still flailed as the wasp scooped up the rest of her body. The other two women were still running as the wasp scurried down the street and grabbed the slower of the two women in its mouth. The woman was tossed around several times inside of the wasp's mouth before she finally died.

The last woman kept running, and she finally made it back to the warehouse. She ran in through the door to the building and slammed it shut behind her. She thought that she was safe until the giant wasp landed on top of the warehouse, where it began tearing through the roof. The group who had remained inside of the warehouse, screamed in terror as the ceiling of their prison began to crumble around them.

A moment later, the wasp penetrated the warehouse and peeked its huge head inside of the building to see the remaining six women huddled in the corner praying that the oversized insect would not be able to enter the building. The wasp pushed its way into the building when it was suddenly pulled backward. There was a loud crash as the wasp landed in the parking lot.

The gathered women ran to the large warehouse windows to see what had happened to the wasp. As they reached the window the ground shook as if a bomb had hit the parking lot. They looked through the window to see the dark form of Ogre standing next to the wasp. Ogre threw his muscular arms back and bared his long fangs as he roared at the creature that had dared to attack his possessions. Ogre was only about a third the size of the wasp, and the giant insect scurried to what it thought would be an easy meal. When the wasp reached Ogre the humanoid creature delivered a punch to the insect's face with such force that the bug's entire head exploded. Ogre roared in triumph, and then he lumbered over to the loading bay doors and into the warehouse itself.

Ogre may have slain the giant wasp but Erin's escape attempt had opened a Pandora's Box. Numerous other giant bugs and animals had seen the prisoners run out of the warehouse, and then back into it. The mutants now knew that there was food located in the building. From that point on, the giant mutants would attack the warehouse on nearly a daily basis. It was at that point, that two factions formed between the remaining five women. The group that consisted of Kim Jones, Maureen Kind, and Kristen Marquette still wanted to try and escape from Ogre. The other two women, Kate Summers and Dinah Long, had resigned themselves to the fact that living under Ogre's oppressive rule was their best chance of survival.

Kim's group continued Erin's plan of tracking Ogre's movements. Kim felt strongly that the time had come to make their move and try to escape from Ogre. Kim was taking one last shot at convincing Kate and Dinah to make the run with them. "Look this time last year Ogre was gone for nearly three days. When he came back he had the carcasses of several dead bison. The bison migrate with the seasons. The herd must be at its farthest point from here right now, and that is why Ogre is gone for so long. This is our chance. We can make it away from that monster."

Kate pleaded with her fellow captive, "Get out of here and do what? Run until some other giant mutant eats us or until we starve to death? Get away from here and only find food that has been affected by radiation?" She placed her hand on Kim's shoulder. "Look, I want to get away from Ogre as much as you do, but we need to wait for help to come for us."

Kim threw Kate's hand off of her. "Wait for help? Wake up, Kate, the apocalypse *has* happened. There is no one coming to help us! We are the only people that can do anything for us."

Kate began to cry. "Then this is all that we have. I hate Ogre as much as any of you, but at least he protects us and feeds us. Where are we going to go that is better than the hell that we are in here?"

Kim shrugged. "I don't know, but at least it will be hell on our terms. I say that it's better out there than being trapped in here like we are Ogre's pets."

Kim turned to her friends. "The mistake that Erin made was actually *running*. We need to move slowly from building to building. By darting in and out of buildings, we won't attract any of those other mutants." Kim grabbed her two friends by their hands. "There are thousands of abandoned cars and trucks out there. All we have to do is find one that works, and then we can drive out of here and leave Ogre behind us forever."

Kim led her friends out of the warehouse as Kate and Dinah watched them take their shot at freedom and the uncertainty that it offered. Kim's plan of moving from building to building was working. The occasional giant bug would fly overhead but they didn't seem to notice the three women as they ducked in and out of doorways and windows. Kate watched as Kim ran from car to car trying to hotwire it. She had tried roughly ten different cars until she got a pick-up truck to turn over. She waved to her friends to jump into the back of the truck. Maureen and Kristin jumped into the pickup and they took off. A giant beetle ran after the truck, but it was too fast for the bug.

As Kate watched the truck drive away part of her wished she had gone with Kim and the others. Two days had passed, with no sign of Ogre, and both Kate and Dinah began to wonder if they had made the wrong choice by staying behind. Kate's mind began to wander as she thought about Kim and the others pulling up to a military stronghold where they were greeted by soldiers with cooked food and clean water. Her daydream was ended when the entire building shook as Ogre came crashing down into the parking lot. The ebony shaded beast entered the warehouse, and he dropped two dead bison onto the floor.

Then Ogre took a long look around the warehouse. When he was unable to locate Kim and the others he roared and shook his head in anger. Ogre ducked back out of the warehouse, and then he leapt off in the direction that Kim had driven.

Kate and Dinah were left alone for a day during which they did their best to carve up the bison. Kate had become pretty good at starting a fire using some of the dried paper and empty wooden skids in the warehouse. Kim was roasting a side of bison when Ogre slammed down into the parking lot. Kate could hear a woman screaming, and a second later, Ogre wandered into the warehouse with Kim screaming in one hand and the dead bodies of Kristen and Maureen hanging in his other hand. He put Kim down, and then he placed the dead bodies next to the door. Kate went over to move the bodies of her friends outside, but Ogre slammed his fist in front of her. She quickly got the message that the monster wanted the bodies left by the door as a reminder that there was no escape from his den.

Kim fell to her knees and broke down in tears. Kate slowly walked over to her and hugged her as Kim wept. "There is no escape from that monster. We are going to live the rest of our lives with him watching over us. We are his prisoners from now until we die." Kim continued to cry as Kate silently held onto her.

CHAPTER 5

After a brief stop at a warehouse in Colorado, Steel Samurai had finally reached California. The robot cleared the mountains outside of Los Angeles, just ahead of the rising sun. Chris had the mech land on the outskirts of the city. He sat in his robot while he took a deep breath and considered his course of action one more time. He knew that this was likely a suicide mission. He was likely never going to return from this endeavor and that thought scared him. In fact, it scared him more than anything else that he had every attempted. Despite his fear about his quest, he had resolved himself to go through with his mission. He would have liked to have convinced himself that it was sheer bravery that helped him to overcome his fear. He would have liked to be able to look deep inside of himself and have found the strength to overcome the challenge before him. If there were other people around him, if there was still some semblance of society left, he might have convinced himself of this because it would help him to convince other people that he was a brave man.

With no one else around, Chris had the burdened of knowing the full truth of his actions. While he was afraid of the consequences of his mission, it was the greater fear of waiting to die at the hands of the monsters that moved him. Just like the nerdy kid who knows that a bully is going to beat him up will challenge the bully just to avoid the apprehension of the coming beating; for this same reason Chris was attacking the kaiju. While he was afraid of dying he was even more afraid of simply being afraid. He was more afraid of the constant threat of the kaiju than he was of the kaiju themselves. Chris was not going to continue to live in constant fear. He was going to take the fight to them and one way or another it would be over. There was one thing that Chris had over the nerdy kid: The nerdy kid hoped against all odds that he could beat up the bully, while Chris was going to get one bully to beat up another.

Chris's thoughts were cut short when the sun finally cleared the mountains behind him to reveal the skyline of the City of Angles.

He had seen the city once before and the magnificent view of L.A. had stuck with him for his entire life. The scene that had brought him so much wonder as a child now filled his mind with horror.

When the sun touched the tops of the buildings he got his first glimpse of the large ants that were crawling around on the tops of the structures. As the sun swept down the rest of the buildings of the L.A. skyline it revealed ants crawling over every street and building in the city. The entire city of Los Angeles looked like one of those ant hills that Chris used to see on the Discovery Channel where a big mound of dirt was blanketed in colored ants. Chris smiled a little when he wished that a giant anteater would come walking by and take out the Colony for him. But fate would not be so kind as to send in a monster to eat the ants. He knew that the setting into motion of the events that would lead to the Colony's destruction was entirely up to him.

Chris brought up all of the information that he had on the Colony from Steel Samurai's data banks. Most of the ants in the colony were about four meters high and six meters long. Steel Samurai was more than ten times the height and weight of each of the ants. The issue was that Steel Samurai was only one mech, while the ants of the Colony were legion. Chris could see thousands of giant ants crawling over the remains of the city, and the robot's sensors detected tens of thousands of more ants in the subway system and tunnels beneath the city. With their increased size the ants all maintained their proportional strength. Each of the creatures was able to lift a thirty ton bulldozer over its head, and their pincers were more than powerful enough to tear through Steel Samurai's hide as if it were cardboard.

There was no possible way that Chris could defeat the countless ants that ruled L.A., but he did not need to defeat them. He only needed to capture one of them. Chris needed to find the Queen Ant. Once he had her in his possession she would send out a call for help that would bring the rest of the Colony scrambling to rescue her. The Queen would be his personal pied piper, and she would single handedly lead the Colony that she ruled over to its doom. Chris's plan to deal with the Colony consisted of four steps. The first step was to retrieve the large barrel of sugar from the abandoned bakery in Boulder, Colorado. That part had been fairly easy. The next step was to place a homing device in the tracker and to drop it in the middle of L.A. The bag would no sooner hit the ground than members of the Colony would spring on it, and then bring it back to the Queen. Once the tracker stopped moving Chris would have his target's location. Then would come the hard part.

Chris would not only have to fight through the heart of the Colony to reach the Queen, he would also have to blast his way through the L.A. underground. An operation like that would take a little bit of time and a lot of concentration. He was well aware that the Colony was unlikely to afford him either of those luxuries. Before the apocalypse, Chris had seen numerous nature shows where a well armored beetle would wander into an ant colony and the ants would tear the larger more powerful beetle to shreds. That same fate could soon be awaiting both Steel Samurai and himself. However, if he could survive the onslaught and reach the Queen, he would nearly be assured his victory because once he had the Queen the other ants would follow her to their doom.

Chris climbed out of his control chair and walked over to the large store of sugar that he had taken from Colorado. He used his knife to pop open the top, and then he slipped in a plastic bag with a homing beacon inside of it. Chris took a deep breath and thought for a long moment before he enacted his plan. Three years ago, before embarking on a difficult mission, he would have said a prayer to God and that would have comforted him. He had ardently believed in God up until the kaiju overran humanity and billions and billions of prayers to God went unanswered. Two years ago Chris had stopped believing in God because the world around him had convinced him that the only thing that there was to believe in was the kaiju and the inevitable death that they represented.

Chris still did not believe in God, and he did still believe in the kaiju, but they were not the only thing that he believed in anymore. Chris was starting to believe in himself. He knew that he was just a man. He was not an all knowing deity or a seemingly all powerful kaiju, he was just Chris Myers. All that he could do was to be the best man that he could be and hope that it was enough to make a difference. Chris closed his eyes as he spoke to himself, "All right,

Chris. It's time to put all thoughts of doubt behind you. You may go down, and you may die, but at least it will be on your terms. You will go down taking the fight to those dammed monsters instead of waiting for them to get you."

Chris pushed his cargo over to the loading dock, and then he walked back to the Steel Samurai's cockpit. Chris took a long hard look at the ants swarming over the skyline that he had so fondly remembered as a child, and then he sent Steel Samurai flying toward the city.

Steel Samurai was nearly over the heart of the city when he dumped the barrel of sugar onto the crawling ants below him. He was pleased to see that the drum had landed in the middle of one ant's head and crushed it. He said aloud, "One down and one hundred thousand to go." Chris kept the mech hovering well above the city as another ant pulled the steel drum out of his brother's crushed head and dutifully began taking it back to his queen. The ant carried the drum to a nearby subway entrance, and then it quickly descended into the L.A. underground. Chris held his breath for a moment as he watched the ant go down into the subway. He was unsure that the beacon's signal would still be able to reach Steel Samurai when it was deep in the subway system. Chris breathed a small sigh of relief as the beacon continued to transmit even after the ant had made it underground.

Chris brought up a schematic of the L.A. subway system, and he watched as the ant quickly traveled through the vast tunnels until it reached the central hub. Chris thought that it made sense that the Queen would be there. She would need room to lay all of her eggs, and the central hub would provide the most space in the subway system. Chris had Steel Samurai fly over directly over the central hub. The hub was nearly ten meters below ground, which meant that the mech had a good deal of digging to do before it even reached the Queen.

The entire ground over the central hub was literally crawling with giant ants. As Chris looked down at the area that he would need to go through, he saw a sea of moving black as the giant ants climbed over each other on their way to carry out their various functions. First, Chris prepared Steel Samurai's defenses as best as he could. The mech had the ability to send a powerful electric shock around its hull in case it was caught in the grip of a kaiju. While the shock was designed to be a quick burst, Chris had modified it to be a steady stream. The stream would not be as powerful as the burst. In fact, Chris doubted that it would even kill the ants when they attacked him, but he at least hoped that it would be enough to slow them down. This was only the first step in his insane mission, and limiting the damage to Steel Samurai was critical. There was no way to repair damage to the mech, and there was no one else to pick up the torch if Steel Samurai were to fail. So keeping the mech in working order was just as important to Chris as was taking out kaiju.

With the electrical field around Steel Samurai functioning as well as it could, Chris aimed two of his most powerful missiles at the area directly above the central hub. Chris gritted his teeth, and then sent the missiles rocketing toward his target. The area below Steel Samurai exploded sending both concrete and parts of giant ants flying off into the sky. Chris didn't wait for the smoke to clear he, simply flew straight at the explosion, with Steel Samurai firing his flamethrower in front of him. Chris moved the robot's arm from side to side and used the flamethrower like a fiery broom to brush away the ants on either side of the entrance. When he had landed, the sides of the entrance were clear, but an army of ants was crawling out of the crater that Chris had created in the middle of the city. Chris immediately turned his flamethrower on the ants and incinerated countless more ants that had managed to avoid his flame as they began advancing on the mech.

The first wave of ants that reached Steel Samurai were tossed off by the electrical field, but as more and more ants climbed onto the robot, the field was stretched thinner. Chris watched in horror as several ants withstood the force of the electrical field and began tearing into Steel Samurai's hull. Chris realized that he needed to act quickly. He had Steel Samurai dive into the entrance to the central hub, with his flamethrower expelling flames in front of the mech. Chris was only able to get the top half of the giant mech into the subway system, and he only got the briefest glimpse of the bloated Queen before his view was filled with the bodies of hundreds of giant ants. Chris heard the sound of metal bending, and he desperately used his controls to have Steel Samurai reach out for the Queen. Chris had Steel Samurai close its grip when he was sure that the mech had grabbed something. He hoped against hope that it was the Queen in the robot's grasp.

Chris backed the mech out of the central hub and onto the streets of L.A. Steel Samurai was completely covered in giant ants as Chris had the robot take to the air once again. When he reached six thousand feet, Chris began using Steel Samurai's free hand to clear the giant ants off of the robot. When he brushed away the ants he was thrilled to see the grotesque form of the Queen securely gripped in the robot's right hand. Once all of the ants were cleared off of Steel Samurai, Chris punched in a flight pattern that would take him to Mexico and straight into Amebos's territory.

Chris had about eighteen hundred kilometers to cover, but he needed to fly at a speed that would allow the Colony to follow him. Holding onto the Queen would not be a problem. The massive ant was nearly half the size of Steel Samurai, but the creature was virtually defenseless. All that she could do was send out a call for help to her followers, and that was exactly what Chris wanted her to do. Chris started flying at speed that would cover the distance to Mexico in two hours. As the robot was flying Chris made sure to keep close tabs on the ants below him. During the flight Chris could not help but to feel a little pride in himself. The first part of his plan had worked. Soon the Colony would be destroyed and L.A. would no longer be under the control of monsters.

Time had passed much more quickly than Chris had realized, and before he knew it, he was flying over what was formerly Mexico. Steel Samurai's sensors were quickly able to locate Amebos. The mech flew over the gel-like monstrosity where it held its position. Chris looked down at the writhing horror that was Amebos. The creature looked like a livening mass of jelly. Long tentacle like extensions stretched out from the formless beast as it sensed the organic material that was the Queen above it. Amebos was hungry, and the Queen would provide it with the genetic material that the formless beast required to survive. When Chris looked over the horizon he could see an endless river of black moving directly toward Amebos. Chris smiled to himself at the sight of the Colony as he said, "All right you ugly piece of crap, its feeding time."

With that, Steel Samurai dropped the Queen directly on top of Amebos. The Queen splashed down into the creature's body where Amebos's enzymes began to dissolve her body. The Queen cried out to her Colony for help until her head slipped into Amebos and she was finally killed. The rest of the Colony were still following their Queen's orders, and they rushed headlong into the writhing form of Amebos; and as each ant was starting to be dissolved by the horror it, called out to its brothers for help.

Chris landed Steel Samurai a safe distance from Amebos and he did nothing but watch for two hours as the creature absorbed every last member of the Colony.

CHAPTER 6

Egg Harbor, New Jersey

Atomic Rex stood directly in front of the glowing crack in the nuclear reactor. The kaiju's unique cells had soaked up as much radiation as they could, and the beast was ready to move on. He sniffed the air, and as he did so, he could smell the salty wind of the nearby ocean. The monster had satiated his need to consume radioactive energy, but he was still a living creature and required food as well as radiation to sustain his body. Atomic Rex was as equally at home in the water as he was on land. Driven by the hunger in his stomach, the kaiju started making his way toward the Atlantic Ocean.

The creature walked for roughly half an hour before he came to the beach. Atomic Rex stopped and looked over the vast stretch of ocean that he also considered his territory. The monster took frequent trips to the ocean, not only for food, but simply to immerse himself in the warm waters of the Atlantic Ocean. Atomic Rex took a step into the water and the gnawing in his stomach quickly intensified. When the kaiju had first claimed the Northeastern United States as his territory he had found the land to provide far more food than the ocean. He was able to catch the occasional whale to help sustain but there was not an abundance of sea creatures that were large enough to satisfy the nuclear dinosaur. Within a year, Atomic Rex soon found that there were huge forms of sea life suddenly appearing in his waters. He also noticed that these creatures were increasing in number as well as size. The increase in oversized sea life was due to Tortiraus's presence in the Gulf of Mexico. The radioactive turtle was causing the sea life in the Gulf to mutant into giants. These giants would in turn follow the Gulf Stream along the east coast and directly into the waters where Atomic Rex hunted.

Atomic Rex continued to wade out into the ocean until his body was fully submerged. The kaiju moved his powerful tail from side to side, and it propelled him through the water at speeds never dreamt of by man and his machines. Atomic Rex could sense the electrical impulses of all the creatures within the water near him. Everything from small shrimp scurrying along the ocean floor, to a large Beluga Whale swimming ahead of him, was picked up by the creature's enhanced senses.

Atomic Rex's mind sifted through the information being sent to him when he finally locked onto a target several kilometers ahead of him. The prey was dangerous even for Atomic Rex. It was in deep waters, and despite his ability to swim through the ocean, he still needed to breath. The prey that the kaiju stalked was strong and capable of drowning Atomic Rex. More importantly, this prey was also a predator, and it would be hunting Atomic Rex just as Atomic Rex was hunting it.

Atomic Rex briefly surfaced and took a deep breath of air. The kaiju then descended back underneath the waves. He immediately detected that the prey was heading for him. The creature was going to attack him head on. Atomic Rex began to swing his tail from side to side at an increased rate as he picked up speed in response to the oncoming prey. Within the hour, one of these titans would be feasting on a meal that would satisfy his hunger for several weeks and the other beast would be food.

The waters of the Atlantic were dark and murky. Atomic Rex's eyesight was virtually useless but he did not need his sense of sight to know the location of the other beast. He could feel the electrical impulses given off by its heartbeat. As the two monsters drew closer to each other, Atomic Rex could sense where the other beast was in relation to him. What he was unable to sense, however, was exactly how large the beast was, because its size seemed to be constantly changing. The question of the creature's size was quickly answered when three tentacles shot out and wrapped around Atomic Rex. The nuclear dinosaur felt the tentacles beginning to constrict on his tail, his torso, and his left arm. With its grip firmly secured, the giant octopus pulled the rest of its bulk onto Atomic Rex. The octopus was colossal. It was nearly twice the size of Atomic Rex. Atomic Rex tried to shake loose from the larger monster's grip, but his convulsions only caused the hook like appendages within the octopus's suckers to dig deeper into the scales of the kaiju.

Atomic Rex felt his body being simultaneously cut and crushed. The kaiju could also feel that the struggle was quickly burning up the air within his lungs. Atomic Rex took his right claw and gashed the octopus across its bulbous head. He then shot forward with his jaws and bit off the tentacle wrapped around his tail. Despite the damage to its body, the giant octopus continued to press its attack by wrapping a tentacle around each of Atomic Rex's legs. The octopus then dropped its body to the ocean floor like a huge anchor as it attempted to use its weight to wear Atomic Rex down.

Atomic Rex could feel that his air supply was nearly exhausted, and once more the monster's will to survive drove him to attack with increased ferocity. The kaiju plunged his right claw deep into the head of the cephalopod, and then he pulled the octopus to within reach of his powerful jaws. With one bite, Atomic Rex tore the pulpy head of the octopus in half. The tentacles of the octopus tightened around Atomic Rex's body, and then with no more input from the brain, the tentacles slowly went limp.

Atomic Rex gulped down the large chunk of octopus in his mouth as he quickly swam to the surface. The kaiju breached the water and took a deep breath of life giving air. He floated on the surface and took several more deep breaths before submerging once more to claim his kill.

As Atomic Rex swam back toward the slain octopus, he saw a colossal crab approaching the dead cephalopod. When it saw Atomic Rex the giant crab backed away from the remains, content to let Atomic Rex eat his fill before moving in for the leftovers. With the acquiescence of the crab, Atomic Rex settled down next to the octopus and began devouring the remains of his former adversary.

The giant crab sat silently on the ocean floor as two more of his kind crawled up next to him and settled down as well.

CHAPTER 7

Santa Fe

Kate rolled over for what seemed like the hundredth time as the sun began to shine through the warehouse windows. She had not slept for nearly three days. Her entire body ached from lying on the cement floor of the warehouse. What little linens that were in the warehouse three years ago had long since been torn to shreds. Within a year, Ogre's captives were left with nothing to sleep on but the cold hard floor. Additionally, what was left of her clothing, as well as the clothing of Kim and Dinah, was ripped to pieces too. So that when they tried to sleep on the floor it was often with their exposed skin directly on the concrete. The result was that the slightest movement cut and bruised them. Kate's body was covered with scratches, scars, and cuts which made sleeping nearly impossible.

Aside from being uncomfortable, there was the horrible smell that permeated the warehouse. Ogre was sleeping next to the warehouse doors by the bodies of Kristen and Maureen. The beast was lying on his side as drool poured over his fangs and onto the floor. The odor coming from the monster smelled like an animal pen at a zoo which had not been cleaned in years. It was the combined smell of sweat and fetid breath.

As if Ogre's smell was not horrible enough, there were also the rotting bodies of Maureen and Kristen. It had been almost two weeks since Ogre had killed them for trying to escape. The monster had also placed them near the door of the warehouse as a reminder to the other women of what would happen to them if they tried to escape. The bodies of the two women had grown bloated, and they were infested with flies. The smell was overwhelming, and the sight of the bodies was gruesome.

During the three years they had been prisoners of Ogre, Kate had grown closer to the women that she was trapped with than she had been with anyone else before the coming of the kaiju. Kate had come to look at her fellow captives as more than friends, even more than family. As far as Kate knew, the other women were the only living humans on the planet. That thought created a bond stronger than any other relationship that she had previously had, and to see Kristen and Maureen dead and rotting a few feet away from her, was more than she could bear.

It was clear to Kate that a deep depression had set in on Kim. She blamed herself for the deaths of Kristen and Maureen. She also believed that it was her fault that Ogre had sentenced them to live in the same building as the decaying bodies of their former friends. Kim was barely eating and her already thin body had withered to the point where she looked like a woman stricken with anorexia. She ate and drank just enough to sustain herself, while otherwise being totally withdrawn. Since the escape attempt she had not spoken to either Kate or Dinah. She was currently sitting against the wall with her knees pulled up to her chest as she stared at the flies jumping onto and off of the bodies of Kristen and Maureen.

Dinah was holding up about as well as Kate under the oppressive rule of Ogre. Dinah ate and drank enough water to keep herself relatively healthy, but the stress of the situation was wearing on her too. Like Kate, she was now virtually naked and covered with cuts and bruises. She had also gone several days without sleep, and the lack rest was taking its toll on her body. Dinah sat on some crates and stared out the window at the rising sun. She did all that she could to avoid looking at Ogre and the bodies of Kristen and Maureen.

Kate had come to look at Dinah as the only remaining person that she could talk to. Dinah was Kate's last remaining anchor to sanity and the will to survive. Kate began walking toward Dinah to talk to her. She had no idea what she was going to say. She only knew that she needed some kind of human interaction. Kate had almost reached the windows when Dinah screamed out in terror.

Kate ran over to the windows and climbed up on the boxes that she and the others had piled up. When Kate reached the top of the boxes she looked out and saw three praying mantises, each standing well over forty meters tall. The mantises were closing in on the warehouse, with their long claw like appendages extended out in front of them. Kate was sure that the mantises were planning to attack the warehouse. As much as she despised the idea of going to Ogre for anything, she knew that she needed to wake the monster up so that he could protect them from the approaching mutants.

Kate ran over and starting yelling at Ogre. The beast opened his eyes briefly, and then he rolled away from Kate and went back to sleep. Kate cursed in frustration. She knew Ogre was a heavy sleeper. It was entirely possible that Ogre would not wake up until the giant mantises had torn up half of the warehouse and crushed Kate, Dinah, and Kim in the process. She yelled at Ogre one more time in vain, and then she began forming a plan to wake the sleeping giant. "Dinah, quick, grab one of the wooden skids that we use for cooking and drag it over to Ogre!"

Dinah immediately jumped down from the windows and went running to grab a skid. As Dinah was going for the skid, Kate was frantically running through the warehouse looking for scraps of paper, cloth, or insulation. She grabbed anything that she could which would help her start a fire. In the three years that they had been living in the warehouse, most of the scraps of paper that they could find had been used up. She was forced to pull some insulation from a crack in the wall in order to start the fire. He fingers were cut and the stinging pink insulation worked its way into the wound as Kate probed the interior of the wall for the kindling that she needed to wake the beast, who was both her jailer and protector. Kate pulled her bleeding hand out of the wall as Dinah dragged a skid over toward Ogre. Dinah placed the skid next to Ogre's face, and then she began screaming at the creature, "Wake up you ugly monster! It's one of the few times that we actually need you, and you are going to sleep right through those bugs eating us!"

One of the mantises peered in through the warehouse window as Kate smashed two rocks together causing sparks to fly off them. She cursed with each strike as sparks fell onto the insulation but failed to ignite it. The insulation finally caught fire as the mantis outside of the building used his claw to shatter the window.

Glass sprayed over Kim, who simply sat there staring at the remains of Maureen and Kristen, as shards of glass cut her arms and face.

Kate and Dinah ran to the far side of the warehouse, away from the mantis, as the fire from the insulation jumped onto the wooden skid.

The mantis stuck his head into the window as the skid burst into flames. The smoke and fire from the skid finally woke the sleeping Ogre. Ogre shook his head, and then he turned to see the mantis reaching in with its claw toward the motionless and bloody Kim. Ogre stood, and his massive body smothered the very fire that had been used to wake him. The monster roared at the mantis, and then he launched himself into the creature's midsection. The force of Ogre's attack pushed the mantis back out of the building.

Ogre bounced off the giant bug, and he found himself standing in the parking lot staring at not one, but three giant mantises. The mantis that Ogre had pushed out of the warehouse struck at Ogre, with his claw, and the blow sent the smaller creature flying into the outer wall of the warehouse. Ogre slid down the wall, and then stood enraged at the creature that had tried to hurt him. Ogre jumped and landed on the mantis's face. Ogre began to pound one mantis while the other two mutants started tearing what was left of the roof off the warehouse.

Inside the building, Kate and Dinah hid behind some of the metal shelving left over from when the building was a functioning warehouse. They screamed for Kim to join them, but the depressed woman simply refused to move from where she was.

One of the mantises saw the bodies of Maureen and Kristin lying by the warehouse doors. The creature skewered the bodies on it claw and began lifting them up to its mouth, when Kim suddenly stood and sprinted toward the remains of her fallen friends.

Kim grabbed onto the leg of Maureen's body. "No! You can't have them! They are mine! They are my responsibility!"

The added weight of Kim's emaciated body made no difference to the giant mantis. It simply put Kim into its mouth with the deceased bodies of her friends.

Kate and Dinah covered their ears and began to cry when they heard Kim's screams of pain and despair as the monster ate her alive. Kim's body was simultaneously being torn apart and crushed together with the remains of her dead friends while she was still alive.

Outside of the warehouse, Ogre struck the head of the mantis that he battled until its exoskeleton gave way and its face caved in. The giant mantis fell to the ground with Ogre still holding onto its smashed face. When the mantis hit the pavement, Ogre looked toward the warehouse to watch Kim scream one last time before the mantis chewing on her finally swallowed her.

Ogre roared in anger that another one of his pets had been taken from him. He jumped toward the mantis that had eaten Kim and he struck the giant insect in the leg—snapping the appendage in two. The mantis hobbled backward as its companion continued to root through the warehouse in search of Kate and Dinah.

The mantis whose leg Ogre had torn off regained his balance, and then he struck at the pitch-black beast, with his claw. The blow caught Ogre on the top of his head and drove him into the ground. Ogre was crawling out of the crater that he had created when the giant mantis struck him again—driving him even deeper into the ground.

Ogre looked up to see the huge claw coming down at him for a third strike but this time the ebony mutant was ready for the attack. Ogre reached up and grabbed the claw before it struck him. With strength beyond comprehension, Ogre pulled on the mantis's claw and tore it from the insect's body. The injured insect staggered away from Ogre, turned, spread its wings, and took off in flight away from the beast that had injured it. Ogre roared at the fleeing mantis, and then jumped into the air after it. Ogre landed on top of the mantis and he dug one of his hands into the insect's back. With his free hand, Ogre reached up and grabbed the quickly moving wing of the mantis, and then he ripped the insect's wing off as easily as he had its claw and leg.

With one of its wings missing, the giant mantis began to plummet back to Earth. It crashed into the building that had at one point been Santa Fe's town hall. The mantis was trying to lift its injured body out of the rubble when Ogre climbed up its back and put his fist through the rear of the mantis's head.

With another opponent defeated, Ogre looked back to his den to see the third giant mantis collapse the south wall of the warehouse.

The last of the giant mantises was using its long claw to probe the interior of the warehouse. Kate and Dinah watched from behind the flimsy shelter of the steel shelving as the claw crushed skids, boxes, and few stray desks. The mantis's claw smashed through several cubicles, and then it veered directly for the shelving that Kate and Dinah hid behind. The two women screamed and tried to run, but Dinah tripped in front of Kate. Fighting against her instincts to run, Kate reached down to help Dinah up. The loss of her forward motion cost her too much time as the steel shelving fell on both Kate and Dinah—pinning the two women to the floor.

Kate looked up to see the giant mantis's ravenous gaze peering down at her. She screamed when she saw the long green claw of the insect reaching down to impale her and Dinah. Kate was about to close her eyes from the horror when a dark, black projectile slammed into the mantis's head.

Ogre struck the giant insect directly on its left eye, causing the organ to exploded and gush out a thick yellow fluid. Ogre then dropped to the mantis's thorax where he stuck the creature again with enough force to stagger it backward. The giant mantis was trying to regain its balance when Ogre crawled around to the back of the mantis. The monster dug his clawed hands into the neck of the insect, and then he pulled up tearing the mantis's head off its body. Blood from the creature sprinkled down into the warehouse. A droplet of the blood flew past Kate and Dinah, but thankfully the drops missed hitting the two women directly.

Ogre roared and shook the head of his kill for about two minutes before he threw it into the parking lot. He then jumped down into the remains of the warehouse, lifted the steel shelving off of his trapped pets, and tossed it outside. Ogre looked briefly at his two remaining pets. He grunted at them, and then the monster wandered outside where he began to devour the head of the last giant mantis that he had killed.

Dinah grabbed Kate and hugged her. "Thank God we made it through all of that. I thought for sure we were going to die."

As Kate looked at the gaping hole on the far side of the warehouse and the radioactive blood splattered across the floor, she was not so sure that they had made it through the attack alive. She pulled Dinah off her and pointed to the blood around the warehouse. "We need to get as much fresh water as we can to try and wash that blood away. For all that we know it still has enough radiation in it to kill us. Once that's done we need to stack everything that we can in that opening. Without the wall, there is nothing to protect us from the next attack. We may as well be sitting outside and waiting for something to eat us."

Kate took a quick look around the warehouse taking inventory of what they still had left. She quickly decided on a course of action and relayed it to Dinah, "The first thing that we are going to do is lay a foundation of insulation in the opening. Then we are going to stack as many of the remaining skids as we can on top of it." Kate sighed as she considered the implications and the limited scope of her plan. "Whenever Ogre is hunting or sleeping we need to take turns watching the opening. If we see a monster heading for us we need to quickly ignite the kindling. Hopefully it will catch fire quick enough to make a firewall, and it will be enough to keep the monster out until Ogre gets back or we can escape."

Dinah shook her head as she heard the words coming from Kate. "What if the fire spreads and we get trapped in the burning warehouse? What if the next monster just flies or jumps over the flames? What if we can't get the fire started quick enough?" Dinah began to shake. "Even if the firewall does work, what do we do the time after that? We only have enough skids to make that kind of wall once. What about cooking our food? If we use the skids to make the wall how will we cook the beef that Ogre brings?"

Kate grabbed Dinah by the shoulders. "Dinah, I don't know. Okay? All I do know is that the first thing that we need to do is get that blood out of here so that we don't die of radiation poisoning. All of your questions about the firewall are valid but none of them will matter if we let a giant centipede crawl in here and eat us while Ogre is out hunting. Let's clean up this blood and see if we can't come up with another plan. If we can't think of anything better to do we will set up the firewall and answer all of those other questions when we get to them."

Dinah shook her head, and then Kate began leading her back to the sink where they got their fresh water from. Kate was trying to look strong for Dinah's sake, but she had the exact same fears that Dinah did. With the wall gone, Kate was fully aware that the only thing between them and the mutants of the world was Ogre.

Without the walls, they were fully exposed to the horrors outside of the warehouse. Kate knew the attacks would soon increase in frequency, and eventually, an attack would come when Ogre was not around. She also knew that at best she and Dinah had a few weeks left to live, and in the worst case scenario, they would be dead by sunset.

CHAPTER 8

Los Angeles

The alarm that Chris had set to go off six hours after he had laid down inside the cabin of Steel Samurai woke the pilot from the most refreshing sleep he had in years. Steel Samurai had landed in the middle of Los Angles, and with the recent extermination of the Colony, there was not another living thing anywhere nearby. Most of the other giant mutants feared the Colony and as such they steered clear of Los Angles. So with the Colony gone, Chris was able to sleep without fear of Steel Samurai being attacked, and without the apprehension of someone knocking on his door to deal with some threat to the settlement.

Chris stretched briefly, and then walked over to the small shower inside of Steel Samurai. Since the robot was nuclear powered, and because it was constantly battling radioactive monsters, the mech had a small shower system filled with fresh water that Chris used to wash regularly as a precaution against radiation poisoning.

As Chris showered he considered how his peaceful sleep gave validation to the mission that he had decided to embark on. If everyone in the settlement could go to sleep without worrying about attacks from giant monsters their lives would be infinitely improved over their current existence. They could live without fear, and the lack of constant fear would lead to hope. Chris was sure of this because his victory over the Colony had given him hope that his mission could succeed. That hope in turn invigorated him to continue his mission. For the first time since the human race had lost the Northeast to Atomic Rex, Chris felt that he could make a difference in the world.

Chris dried off, and then he was eager to start the next phase of his mission. In this case, the next phase of his mission would be to attack Yokozuna and to draw the cannibalistic giant east and into the territory of either of Giladon or Ogre. The path to Giladon's territory would be slightly shorter and would also be a direct path east. Given the size and speed at which Yokozuna moved, Chris figured he could draw the giant into Giladon's territory in about six hours. Conversely it would take him about eight hours traveling in a southeastern direction to draw Yokozuna into Ogre's territory.

Chris considered his options, and after going through multiple scenarios, he decided to lead Yokozuna into Giladon's territory because it was shorter and he could draw the easily angered Ogre into battling the winner. It would also position the monsters in an area where whichever beast came out on top would be in prime position to battle the winner of the Atomic Rex-Dimetrasaurs matchup. Chris also planned to have Tortiraus battle Amebos, and then to draw the winner of that battle north to engage whatever monster was left from the other battles that he was contriving. He still felt strongly that Atomic Rex and Tortiraus would be the last two standing, although in the long run, it really didn't matter as long the majority of the monsters killed each other off. With the rest of his mission mapped out, Chris sent Steel Samurai north heading to the San Francisco Bay area and the gargantuan Yokozuna.

The flight to San Francisco took Steel Samurai less than twenty minutes. Chris circled the city once, but he was unable to locate the giant. Steel Samurai banked back toward the bay when he saw the obese giant sitting in the middle of AT&T Park, home of the San Francisco Giants. The giant was squatting down on all fours and reaching through the concourses of the stadium. Chris figured that a good amount of refugees probably had headed there during his initial attack, and Yokozuna was now picking through the stadium to see if he missed anyone. Chris took a deep breath as he landed Steel Samurai next to the ballpark. Of all of the kaiju that he would be facing he had the most disgust and hatred for Yokozuna. The giant was the one kaiju who actively sought out people in order to eat them. The other monsters killed people, but they did not go out of their way to try and eat humans. The act of consuming people was made even more horrifying when Chris considered that Yokozuna had once been a human himself. Chris did not know how much of the man that had become Yokozuna was still aware within that huge frame, but if there was even the slightest glimmer of the man in the monster, then how could the man let the monster eat his own kind?

Yokozuna rose out from the middle of the stadium when he heard Steel Samurai land next to the building. Yokozuna's face looked like that of a middle aged Polynesian man, except the skin on his face looked as if it had half melted. The giant's brow sloped down over the top part of his eyes in an uneven fashion so that his eyes almost peered out from behind the brow. The lower part of the obese goliath's face was accentuated by no less than four chins.

As he continued to rise, Chris saw the huge gut of the creature that thankfully loped over Yokozuna's waist and covered his genitals. The giant was staring at Steel Samurai when the robot landed a right jab to the giant's face, followed by a roundhouse punch with its left fist.

Yokozuna's face barely moved from the impact of the blows, but the attack did serve the purpose of enraging the kaiju. With a speed that seemed impossible for his size, Yokozuna ran right through the stadium walls and grabbed Steel Samurai in a crushing grip. The giant lifted the mech off its feet, shook it from side to side, and then threw it on the ground. Steel Samurai was thrown to the ground with such force that the street below him cracked.

The mech was lying flat on its back as Chris looked up to see Yokozuna reaching down for him. Chris quickly realized that if Yokozuna were to climb on top of the mech that the giant's immense weight would crush the robot's frame.

Chris hit the ignition button for Steel Samurai's booster rockets, which sent the robot skidding on its back away from Yokozuna. When Chris had cleared roughly a dozen blocks he stopped the mech's progress and stood Steel Samurai upright. Yokozuna bellowed at the robot, and then began to charge at it. Chris's adrenaline was pumping and his initial thought was to charge the giant and meet him head on, but Chris calmed himself and remembered his plan. "No, this is what you want. You want him to follow you. Chris had the robot hover a few feet off the ground, and then he began to head east with Yokozuna pursuing him.

The pursuit had gone on for over an hour when Yokozuna suddenly stopped chasing after Steel Samurai. Chris cursed,

"Come on you fat bastard! Don't give up yet!" Chris armed the high powered machine guns within Steel Samurai's chest. The hatch that held the gun's slide opened, and Chris unleashed a barrage into Yokozuna.

Chris saw the impact of each bullet as it caused an indent in the bulbous gut of the giant. Each bullet sent a wave of fat rolling across the giant's flabby body. Chris turned his head in disgust from the site of Yokozuna absorbing the bullets. Chris kept the barrage relatively short by only firing a couple hundred rounds. He was still well aware that he needed to conserve as much ammunition for the rest of his quest as possible. When Chris ended the burst of gunfire Yokozuna moaned in anger, and the giant started to chase after Steel Samurai once again.

When they had reached the halfway point of the journey Yokozuna again started to give up his pursuit of Steel Samurai. Chris was taking mental notes of how Yokozuna was reacting to Steel Samurai in hopes that he could in some way use the information against the other kaiju that he still needed to face. In Yokozuna's case, he did not seem to feel the need to chase a threat totally out of his territory as long as the intruder seemed to be moving away from him and was acknowledging the giant as the dominant creature in the region. Chris realized that in order to ensure pursuit he would have to increase the frequency in which he attacked the kaiju. He concluded that an attack every three quarters of an hour should be a thick enough frequency to ensure that the kaiju kept up the pursuit. Chris had Steel Samurai draw his sword to attack the giant. He was not fond of the idea of not only engaging Yokozuna at close range again but also every other creature. He figured that maybe once he had thinned the heard some that he could start employing his long range weapons more frequently, but for now, he needed to conserve them.

Steel Samurai flew directly at Yokozuna and slashed the corpulent giant across his chest. The blade penetrated the giant's flesh, but the fat was so thick that the weapon was unable to cut through it to reach organs or bones. Steel Samurai quickly fell to one knee and sliced Yokozuna across his midsection with the same result as cutting his chest.

With one powerful backhand strike, Yokozuna sent Steel Samurai tumbling head over heels across the deserts of Nevada.

Inside of Steel Samurai, Chris was thrown out of the pilot's seat and across the cockpit. He scrambled back to the pilot's chair and brought Steel Samurai back on its feet before Yokozuna was able to grab him. Steel Samurai sliced the giant across his leg and delivered an elbow to his face. Steel Samurai then levitated off the ground, and it continued in an eastward direction. Chris took a look around the cockpit at the nerve center of his robot. "You mechs may not be strong enough to do any real damage to the True Kaiju but you sure as hell can outmaneuver them."

The pursuit continued throughout the night with Steel Samurai attacking Yokozuna with his sword at regular forty-five minute intervals. It was just around 3 a.m., when the monster and mech crossed into the area that had been designated as Giladon's territory. An hour and twenty minutes after they had crossed into Giladon's domain, Chris got a second radar reading on Steel Samurai's control panel. He smiled. "Hey there you are you wanna-be from a cheap horror movie. It's time for you to defend your territory."

It was a full moon night, and Chris was far enough away from Yokozuna to lift his the battle shields off Steel Samurai's eyes so that he could see the landscape for himself. Yokozuna was either too enraged to notice that another kaiju was approaching or he simply did not care. Chris turned Steel Samurai away from Yokozuna to see what was behind him. When Steel Samurai turned around Chris saw a giant quadrupedal creature.

The beast had the overall body and coloring of a Gila Monster. Its body was long and round with white and red stripes alternating across its skin. The creature did have some other aspects to it that were totally different from a typical Gila Monster. At the tip of the creature's snout, there was a long, thick horn. The back end of the kaiju was equally as dangerous, and it condensed into a thick club like tail similar to that of the ancient ankylosaurs. Giladon was roughly sixty meters long and thirty meters tall. The creature was longer than Yokozuna, but it was nowhere near as tall or as heavy as the humanoid giant.

With the two kaiju so close to each other, Chris had Steel Samurai shoot up into the sky and out of the reach of both monsters. Giladon watched Steel Samurai rocket into the heavens. Satisfied that one threat to its rule was gone, Giladon turned his attention to Yokozuna. Giladon slithered forward and hissed at the giant human. Yokozuna moaned, and then stomped his foot on the ground in acceptance of Giladon's challenge. Chris watched from above as the two monsters stared at each other in the light of the full moon.

Giladon hissed one more time, and then the colossal reptile began charging across the desert. When Yokozuna saw Giladon charging at him the obese giant roared, and then he also charged!

CHAPTER 9

Giladon moved much quicker than the behemoth Yokozuna. The reptilian kaiju darted across the desert, and when he reached the giant, Giladon reared up and clamped his jaws around Yokozuna's arm. Yokozuna threw his head back as he was wailing in pain. Yokozuna tried to shake Giladon loose but that only caused the reptile to dig his claws into the giant's bulbous gut. Giladon shook his head from side to side causing his teeth to act like a saw. The slicing motion of Giladon's attack tore even deeper through the layers of fat that covered that giant's organs, veins, and bones.

As Chris watched from above, he sneered, "That's it, tear that fat bastard apart." Chris had no love for Giladon. He wanted the reptile to die just as much he wanted all of the other monsters to die. Chris was pulling for Giladon because he loathed Yokozuna for being the cannibal that he was. Chris watched as Yokozuna delivered a knife-edge chop into the back of Giladon's neck that snapped the monster's jaws free from his arm and sent his face crashing into the ground. Chris shook his head in further disgust. He not only hated Yokozuna for what he was, but he also hated him for what he could have been. Yokozuna kicked Giladon in the face, wrenching the kaiju's head to the side. He then reached down, wrapped his powerful arms around Giladon's midsection, and lifted the monster over his head. Yokozuna slammed Giladon to the ground with a power-bomb style slam, and as Giladon slithered clear of him, the giant roared at his opponent.

Chris watched as Giladon circled back around to continue his attack, while his thoughts continued to focus on the lost potential of Yokozuna. Chris could see that the giant was powerful and easily capable of battling any of the kaiju on equal terms. Chris thought that if even the slightest glimmer of the man who had formerly been Yokozuna was still within the giant then he could have been the savior of mankind! The giant could have fought the kaiju, and he would have been far more successful than the mechs were against the monsters. Yokozuna would have been fed and cared for by the people, instead of being despised by them. Chris took a deep breath because he knew where his true underlying hatred for the giant came from. Chris hated Yokozuna because the giant could have taken this responsibility off his shoulders. Yokozuna could have been the last protector of humanity. He could be the one taking this last effort to try and save mankind by eradicating the monsters that ruled the earth. He could have done those things, but instead, he was a mindless kaiju that ate people. Chris knew that it was unfair to throw all of that on a man who through no fault of his own had become a monster. Still, Chris didn't care. It wasn't like he relished the role that he was trying to fill on behalf of the human race. If he could find a scapegoat to help him deal with the stress of his situation then he was okay with that. It's not like it mattered to Yokozuna.

With his self-therapy session complete, Chris refocused on the battle taking place below him. Giladon seemed to realize that he lacked the strength to simply overpower his opponent. The reptile walked close to Yokozuna, but this time he stopped just short of engaging the giant. Yokozuna roared and then moved forward to attack Giladon once again. When Yokozuna was within range, Giladon spun around and sent his club like tail crashing into Yokozuna's leg. Yokozuna's thick leg was displaced from where it originally was, causing the giant to pitch off balance, and fall onto his left side.

Chris watched as the entire desert shook from the act of the obese giant falling down. With Yokozuna down, Giladon pressed his attack. The kaiju backed up to Yokozuna, and then he brought his thick tail crashing into the giant's face. The giant's head snapped back causing his body to roll so that he was laying on his back and staring up into the night sky. Giladon continued to use his tail to batter Yokozuna. The kaiju's tail slammed into the giant's head, shoulder, and arm over and over again. Chris thought that Yokozuna was finally going to die when his pudgy hand suddenly shot out and grabbed Giladon's tail. Giladon tried to pull free of Yokozuna, but the giant's grip was powerful and there was no way that even Giladon would be able to move the weight of the giant.

The giant slowly stood as he kept his firm grip on the tail of Giladon. When Yokozuna was upright, he placed his other hand on

Giladon's tail and then pulled. The move sent Giladon tumbling across the desert. Once more Chris was astonished at the speed of Yokozuna. The giant dashed across the desert, and when he reached Giladon, he delivered a series of vicious kicks and chops to the monster's head. Giladon's was rocked by each blow that the giant landed on him. Yokozuna lifted his right foot to stomp on Giladon's head, but the reptile used the opportunity to lunged forward and sink his jaws into the giant's left calf. Blood poured into Giladon's mouth as the monster pulled backward, displacing the giant's weight enough to cause him to fall onto his back.

Once more the desert shook as the mass of flesh and bone that was Yokozuna came crashing down onto it. Giladon continued to bite and claw at Yokozuna's left calf until the giant used his left leg to kick Giladon off him. Yokozuna's kick had pushed Giladon back, and he thought that he had enough time to stand before Giladon recovered. Yokozuna realized his mistake as he made it to his knees only to have Giladon drive the horn at the tip of his snout into Yokozuna's stomach.

Blood gushed over Giladon's face, and the monster roared as he continued to drive his horn farther into the giant's gut. Yokozuna was in anguish as he grabbed the horn digging into his flesh.

Within the cockpit of Steel Samurai, Chris clenched his hands. As the blood continued to gush out of Yokozuna, Chris thought to himself that object of his hatred was finally going to die. Chris squeezed his hands tighter as if by doing so he could will Giladon to drive his horn farther into Yokozuna and finally end the cannibalistic horror.

Chris's hopes began to fade when he saw Yokozuna wrap his fat hands around Giladon's face. When his hands were clasped in place over the kaiju's face, Yokozuna began to push Giladon's entire body backward. As Giladon was forced backward his horn was slowly extracted from Yokozuna's stomach. When the horn was completely out of his body Yokozuna moved one of his hands from Giladon's face, and he used it to grip the horn.

Yokozuna leaned his tremendous weight into the horn causing the bony appendage to snap in half. With the horn gone, Yokozuna wrapped his arms around Giladon and once more he lifted the reptile off of the ground and power-bombed him hard onto the desert. Giladon's entire body was jarred by the impact leaving the creature stunned. Yokozuna could see that his opponent was hurt, so he repeated the move of grabbing Giladon and power-bombing him.

Giladon's back slammed into the desert once more, stunning the kaiju. Giladon looked up to see Yokozuna straddling him from above. Yokozuna threw his legs out in front of him causing his gargantuan frame to come crashing down on top of Giladon's chest. The air rushed out of Giladon's lungs, and his legs and tail shot up into the air in response to the unbelievable weight that had dropped onto his body. Yokozuna was sitting on top of Giladon as the kaiju struggled in vain to free himself from under the girth of the massive giant. Gialdon bit down hard on Yokozuna's inner right thigh, and in response, the giant grabbed the reptile by the throat and strangled him.

Chris watched from up above in disbelief at how the battle had turned out. He was sure that Yokozuna was finished when Giladon had impaled him. Now Chris was watching as Giladon's body shook one last time before the kaiju finally expired.

Chris watched as Yokozuna rolled off the body of Giladon. The giant sat next to the corpse of the slain kaiju and stared at it for a moment. Chris nearly vomited when Yokozuna leaned over and took a bite out of Giladon's corpse. Chris shook his head. "That glutton will eat anything, won't he?" He looked down on the giant as it was bent over the fallen Giladon feasting on the creature. Chris's blood was boiling as he looked down at the former man who had devoured so many of his own kind. For a moment, Chris thought to himself that he could end Yokozuna right now. He knew that the giant had defeated several mechs before in direct combat, but Chris could attack the monster unaware. Steel Samurai could drive its sword right through that fat monster's back. Chris was gripping his controls tightly when doubt began to creep into his mind. He had seen Giladon drive his horn deep into Yokozuna's gut only minutes ago but now the bleeding had stopped, and Yokozuna seemed as if the wound had not really injured him all that much. If Steel Samurai were to drive its sword into the Yokozuna and not kill him, things would go bad quickly. At best Steel Samurai would lose its sword, and at worst, the mech would be destroyed and Chris would be dead. The Colony and Giladon would have been disposed of, but the majority of the True Kaiju would still be roaming the earth taking up resources and creating more mutants. Chris knew that a direct attack would be too risky. With Giladon dead, Yokozuna would now claim the kaiju's territory as his own. Even a ravenous eater like Yokozuna would take several days to consume the body of something as huge as Giladon. Tomorrow it would be simple enough to draw the easily angered Ogre close to Yokozuna. As soon as Yokozuna sensed a threat to his meal he would be quick to attack Ogre. The two man-monsters would then fight to the death.

Chris took one more look at Yokozuna. He watched as the giant ripped one of Giladon's ribs out. The giant quickly gnawed any meat off the rib. Once he had devoured any flesh that was connected to the rib, he snapped the bone in half and sucked the marrow out of it.

Chris turned his mech away from the grisly meal taking place below him. He then had Steel Samurai fly north from Yokozuna at top speed for nearly twenty minutes putting several hundred kilometers between himself and the giant. He landed Steel Samurai, and then set the robot's proximity monitors. He figured that he needed a couple hours of sleep before he continued his quest tomorrow. He quickly showered and ate some of the bread that he had taken from the settlement. After seeing Yokozuna consume part of Giladon, the thought of eating almost repulsed him, but he had not eaten in over twenty-four hours. Chris knew that he would need to keep himself in relatively good health if was to complete his quest.

When he had finished eating he pulled up all of the information that he had on Ogre. The monster was last reported being seen in the city of Santa Fe. A couple of reports had the monster staying at a warehouse on the outskirts of the city. Chris reviewed the data on the monster. Ogre was far smaller than the rest of the True Kaiju, but he was known to have torn apart mutants more than four times his size with ease. Ogre was also reported to be highly resistant to injury. When he had first thought of having Ogre battle the winner of the Yokozuna/Giladon confrontation, he thought that the winner would crush Ogre. The more that he read about the beast though the more he began to think that Ogre might actually have a chance of defeating Yokozuna. Chris planned out his course to Santa Fe, and then he shut down his computer. He climbed into bed, and as he closed his eyes, the thought of the relatively small but powerful Ogre clashing with the mountainous Yokozuna filled his mind.

CHAPTER 10

Atlantic Ocean off the Coast of New Jersey

Atomic Rex sank his claws into the rubbery hide of the deceased octopus. He then bit down into the flesh of the creature and pulled up with his mouth, while simultaneously pulling down on it with his claws. The end result of Atomic Rex's effort was another large chunk of octopus that he quickly chewed and swallowed.

The giant crabs that had gathered around Atomic Rex and his kill were growing restless. While the first animal had initially decided to let the mutant dinosaur eat its fill, the creature became disturbed by the appearance of the other crabs. The colossal crustacean had limited thought processes and knew that with the arrival of the other crabs that it meant less food for itself.

The hunger of the first crab quickly won out over its caution. The giant crab scuttled over to Atomic Rex and the slain octopus. The crab reached out with its claw and grabbed a tentacle of the octopus as Atomic Rex reached down to bite it.

Atomic Rex was furious that the crab would try to take his meal. The nuclear theropod sprang forward and drove his head into the middle of the crab's face, pushing the enlarged crustacean backward. The crab reacted on instinct as his claws shot out and grabbed Atomic Rex around his right arm and upper jaw.

Seeing the flurry of action, the other two giant crabs also reacted on instinct. They quickly moved forward and dug their claws into Atomic Rex's right arm and leg, his torso, and his tail. The crabs' claws were sharp and powerful. The jagged appendages cut deep into Atomic Rex's thick hide. The mutant dinosaur's body was racked with sharp pain from where the crabs' claws had pierced his scales. He tried to shake the crabs loose, but the harder that he struggled, the more the crabs dug their claws into him.

When he had begun feasting, Atomic Rex had more than enough oxygen in his lungs to devour the remains of the octopus, but the struggle with the crabs was causing him to burn through his air supply at a much quicker rate. Once again Atomic Rex was faced with the prospect of drowning if he was unable to free himself from the grips of the deep sea giants. His lungs were bursting, and the kaiju knew that he needed air. Atomic Rex made one more attempt to pull himself free of the crabs, but when he was unable to do so, he resorted to his most powerful attack. Atomic Rex's entire body began to glow as he called forth the energy from deep within him. Having recently absorbed the radiation from the nuclear power plant, the kaiju had more than enough radioactive energy to spare.

Atomic Rex's body shook as his Atomic Wave emanated out from within him. The sphere of nuclear energy pushed the giant crabs through the water as if they were nothing more than mere krill. The crabs were hurtling through the water as Atomic Rex made his way to the surface once again. The kaiju's head burst through the surface of the Atlantic, and he expelled the air within his lungs before sucking back in another breath of oxygen. Atomic Rex looked to the shoreline. He knew that he could swim to shore and leave the crabs behind. He had eaten enough of the octopus to fill his stomach. There was no physical need for him to dive back down into the depths to attack the giant crabs again.

As the thought of the crabs attacking him continued to replay itself within the kaiju's mind, his anger at the crustaceans began to grow. The crabs had not only invaded his territory but they had attacked him while he was feeding. Atomic Rex looked to the sky above and roared before taking another breath of air and plunging back down into the depths of the Atlantic Ocean. Atomic Rex had slain the Marsh–Thing for trying to usurp his energy supply, and he would do the same to these giant crabs that had thought to attack him and take his food.

Atomic Rex was streaking through the water when he saw the three crabs greedily picking at the remains of his kill. Atomic Rex dove straight at the crab that was right in front of him. When he reached the crab the kaiju opened his jaws wide and bit down on the area of the shell where the crab's eyes and mouth were located. Atomic Rex felt one of the crab's eyes pop within his mouth as he let his downward momentum carry him over the back of the crab. The kaiju's grip held as the force of the attack pulled the crab off the ocean floor. A moment later Atomic Rex's feet were resting on the bottom of the ocean as he sent the crab flipping through the water in front of him. The huge crab landed helplessly on its back. The crab's claws and legs flailed wildly as Atomic Rex climbed on top of the smooth white underbelly of its shell. Atomic Rex opened his jaws and thrust them into the crab's weaker bottom shell. The kaiju's teeth penetrated the crab's shell easily and Atomic Rex tore a huge chunk out of the crab. The crab's claws and leg continued to try and right its body. Atomic Rex spit the shell out of his mouth and then he looked down into the soft tissue now exposed from the hole in the crab's armor. Atomic Rex thrust his head into the gap he had torn in the crab's shell, and then he grabbed a mouthful of the crab's soft tissue. Atomic Rex pulled his head back, and in doing so, he ripped out most of the crab's guts. The beast's body twitched for several seconds before all signs of life disappeared from the crab.

Atomic Rex turned to the other crabs only to find them lazily feasting on the remains of the octopus. The giant crabs were so engrossed in their meal that they failed to realize the danger they were in. Atomic Rex shot through the water like a torpedo. When he slammed into one of the remaining crabs, he clamped his jaws around the creature's right claw and gripped the crab's left claw below the pincer with his own claws. Atomic Rex bit and tore at the claw in his mouth until he was able to tear it off. He threw the detached appendage down, and then he pulled on the other claw with all of his tremendous strength until the limb popped out of its socket. The now disabled crab was trying to back away from Atomic Rex when the kaiju's jaws shot forward and bit off the crab's eyes. The blind beast was still trying to flee when Atomic Rex put his claws under the crab's shell and flipped it onto its back. Once again, Atomic Rex climbed on top of his downed opponent. This time instead of biting through the crab's shell the kaiju began tearing the crab's legs off. Within seconds, the giant crab was blind, on its back and totally limbless, but still alive. Atomic Rex swam away from the creature well aware that while not dead yet, the threat to its territory was now totally immobile and defenseless. The kaiju would end the crab's misery several days from now when he needed to feed again, but in the meantime, the crab's meat would remain fresh.

The third crab finally seemed to understand the danger that it was in. The massive beast began to crawl away from the kaiju, pulling the remains of the dead octopus with it. Atomic Rex swam to attack the third crab. When he reached the crustacean its claws reached out and grabbed the kaiju by his arm and leg. Atomic Rex glared at the creature and wrapped his claws around the crab's extended pincers. Once more Atomic Rex's body began to glow as he prepared to unleash his Atomic Wave attack. The last time that he had used the attack it had been to push the attacking crabs off him but now it would be used to slay this last threat to his territory. When the wave burst out from Atomic Rex's body it hit the crab with the force of small tactile nuclear weapon.

Beneath the water, the crab could have floated and let the wave simply push him along, in which case the crab would have suffered only a few burns to its outer shell. However, with Atomic Rex holding the crab in place, the effect was devastating. The force of the wave was pushing the crab backward, but the strength of Atomic Rex was holding its body in place. Atomic Rex stared at the crab as its eyes exploded and its shell was stripped off its body. A millisecond later the creature's body yanked free of its claws at the socket. Atomic Rex was still holding onto the claws of the crab as its charred and shattered remains floated through the water in front of him.

The kaiju grabbed the remains of the octopus, and then rose to the surface of the water. Atomic Rex took a breath of air, and then he swam back to the beach. When he reached the beach the kaiju tossed the remains of the octopus onto the sand, and finally, the nuclear dinosaur laid down in the sand. He had fought three battles today to defend his territory, his power source, and his food. Atomic Rex was tired, but between the remains of the octopus and the blind and disabled crab lying at the bottom of the ocean, he would have enough food to last him for several days. The mighty kaiju lifted his head to roar once more letting any potential intruder into his land know that death awaited them. Atomic Rex then returned his head to the soft sand of the beach and quickly fell asleep.

CHAPTER 11

Santa Fe

Kate was on watch as dusk slowly turned to dawn. She and Dinah had finished the firewall a couple of hours ago. Ogre watched them curiously as they stacked wooden skids on top of the insulation that they had pulled from the wall. Once they had finished their work Dinah went to sleep, and Ogre took a long, hard look at Kate before leaping out into the desert to go hunting. Ogre couldn't speak, but the intent behind his glare was clear to Kate. *If she and Dinah attempted to escape then he would track them down.*

It had been roughly an hour since Ogre had left when the sun started to rise over the desert that the collapsed wall of the warehouse now faced. Kate was looking at the rising sun as it began to silhouette a large form. Kate was unsure of what the silhouette was at first, but as the sun continued to rise, it revealed the shape of a giant scorpion. Kate cursed and then began to talk to herself, "Come on, just turn the other way. Please just turn around and head out into the desert."

Despite her pleas the scorpion continued to walk straight for the warehouse. Kate cursed again when she saw how fast the giant scorpion moved. There was no way she and Dinah could outrun the scorpion if it chose to chase them down. Her heart raced and her palms began to sweat as she picked up rocks and struck them over a small pile of insulation that she had set up away from the firewall. The small pile of insulation had been set up so that they could light a small fire to ignite the firewall if they needed to. This way they were ready to light the firewall but at the same time they would not waste it if a potential threat turned away from the warehouse.

The first time that Kate tried to strike the rocks together she was rushing and smashed her fingers between them. She cursed loudly which woke up Dinah.

Dinah rolled over and looked out of the opening to see the scorpion quickly approaching the warehouse. She stood and ran over to Kate. "Light the fire, Kate! Light the fire!"

Kate slammed the two rocks together again sending a series of sparks into the insulation that quickly died out. She hit the rocks together again and gave a direction to Dinah, "I *am* trying to light it. Go grab a piece of broken wood that we can use as a torch to carry the fire from here to the firewall."

Dinah raced out into the warehouse just as Kate sent another set of sparks flying into the insulation. This time the embers smoldered for a few seconds. Kate bent down and gently blew on the cinders, causing the fire to spread across the insulation. A few second later the insulation had caught fire but it was quickly burning itself out. Kate yelled into the warehouse, "Dinah, hurry up with that wood! This fire won't last long."

Dinah had run throughout the entire warehouse before finding the broken leg of an old wooden chair. She grabbed the leg and ran back to the opening in the warehouse wall. When she reached the opening, Dinah saw Kate frantically sprinting back from the firewall with a handful of insulation that she dumped on the quickly dying fire. The added insulation gave the fire new life, and when Kate saw Dinah running up to her with the wooden leg, she grabbed it from her and thrust into the flames.

It took a good thirty seconds for one end of the leg to catch fire. To Kate the thirty seconds felt like a lifetime. She pulled the burning torch from the fire and turned back toward the makeshift firewall. Kate guessed that the scorpion was roughly four football fields away and closing fast. She ran over to the firewall and stuck the torch into the insulation beneath the skids. She started small fires under the skids at four different spots, and then backed away from the burning insulation while praying that the fire was able to ignite the skids and that it would be able to hold back the scorpion.

The fire was just starting to catch onto the skids when the scorpion had closed the distance to roughly one hundred meters. Kate and Dinah backed up to the far end of the warehouse and looked up to see the giant scorpion peering in through the opening in the warehouse. The monster was sticking one of its claws into the opening when the skids finally caught fire and burned the scorpion, forcing it to back away from the flames. The huge arachnid threw its claws and stinger in front of itself in reaction to the burning flames. The monster backed away from the fire but it didn't leave the warehouse. It simply began circling the building looking for another opening that it could utilize to grab the prey inside.

Kate and Dinah watched from inside the warehouse as the giant scorpion circled the building. In her mind, Kate ran through the scenarios facing them. She knew that either the fire would spread to the rest of warehouse and they would be trapped in a burning building; the fire would burnout and the scorpion would have easy access to them; or Ogre would return and battle the scorpion.

She and Dinah sat down on the floor and watched as the firewall continued to burn, knowing that the life of fire could well represent their reaming time on earth.

CHAPTER 12

Utah

The alarm blared waking up Chris an hour before sunrise. He stretched and then did his morning workout routine of push-ups, sit-ups, and cardio on a treadmill that was in the lower decks of Steel Samurai. He treated himself to an apple for breakfast before returning to the cockpit and taking flight toward Santa Fe. As Chris was in flight, the thought of the settlement once more crept into his mind. He was tempted to check on them and see if they were still alive. He also thought that if they were still alive that he could explain his quest to them.

He shook his head. "No, if I go back I am only doing it to make myself feel better by getting validation of my plan from them. If they were attacked then they are already dead, in which case there is nothing that I could do for them anyway. If they are safe then I am only prolonging the length of my quest by making an extra side trip. The best thing I can do for them is to get these monsters to destroy each other as quickly as possible, and then deal with the consequences of my actions afterward."

With his mind made up, Chris decided to take an inventory of his remaining ammunition before engaging Ogre in battle. Chris still had several thousand rounds of high caliber bullets left. He had over two dozen missiles of various formats at his disposal, and several hundred gallons of gasoline to power his flamethrower. For the most part, Chris was pleased at how well he had done conserving his ammunition thus far. With the kaiju that he still had to face, Chris was sure that his stockpile of ammunition would start declining rapidly.

He walked back to the cockpit when Steel Samurai's internal systems alerted him that they were coming up on the city of Santa Fe. He looked out of Steel Samurai to see a long pillar of smoke floating up into the sky. Knowing Ogre's volatile temperament, Chris thought that perhaps Ogre had destroyed something that blew up when he smashed it.

He flew Steel Samurai over to the pillar of smoke to find a giant scorpion poking at the remains of a warehouse that was on fire. Chris had Steel Samurai hover in the sky near the scorpion. There was no need for him to waste his limited resources engaging the colossal arachnid, and he figured that if Ogre was anywhere within the immediate area that he would return soon to drive the scorpion away from his territory.

Ogre held the bodies of two large bison under his arms as he leapt through the desert. He was able to smell the burning fire long before he could see the pillar of smoke in the sky. He was about twenty kilometers outside of Santa Fe when he finally saw the smoke. Ogre followed the pillar of smoke to its source and even his limited mind was able to comprehend that his warehouse was on fire. The thought that his pets were in danger sent Ogre into a frenzy. The monster put the bison carcasses down, and then he doubled his pace toward the warehouse.

Inside the warehouse Kate and Dinah were choking on the smoke and fumes released by the burning skids and insulation. To make matters worse, the fire was starting to burn out. Once the fire had died down enough the giant scorpion would crawl across the smoldering remains of the firewall and devour them. With no other recourse left, Kate fell to her knees and prayed. She prayed for help to come from up above to save her and Dinah from being eaten by the scorpion.

As she was looking through the opening in the top of the warehouse, she thought that she actually did see something in the sky. She risked taking a few steps closer to the firewall and looked up into the smoke filled sky to see a mech hovering in the air. Her heart nearly jumped out of her chest as she ran back to tell Dinah the good news. "Dinah, there is a mech out there! Do you know what that means? Not only are we saved but this means that humanity has survived. The government must have sent a mech to destroy Ogre and save all of the people that he captured."

Dinah took a step forward and looked up into the sky. "Oh God, I see it! We're saved! We're saved!"

Kate wondered why the mech had not yet engaged the scorpion and it was at that point that she realized that the pilot probably did realize that she and Dinah were in the warehouse. Kate pointed to the emergency exit that led to the parking lot. "Dinah, we have to run out into the parking lot so that the pilot can see us. Once he sees us he can protect us from the scorpion."

Dinah nodded, and then she and Kate ran out into the parking lot.

Chris had a blip on his radar screen indicating that a target was approaching from the desert. He checked the size of the object, and when he realized that the target was roughly eight meters tall and jumping across the desert, he smiled. "Hello, Ogre." Chris sent Steel Samurai flying out to engage Ogre just as Kate and Dinah ran into the parking lot. Steel Samurai was flying straight toward the incoming radar signal, and within seconds, Chris could see the dark black form of Ogre leaping into the air. Chris gripped his controls tightly, and adrenaline shot through his veins as he had Steel Samurai pull its sword from the sheath in the robot's leg. Chris knew that he would have to strike hard and move quickly, because in terms of speed, Ogre was able to move far faster than any of the other True Kaiju. Chris knew that as soon as Steel Samurai attacked Ogre that the ebony monster would spring after the mech in pursuit.

Ogre hit the ground, and then once again leapt back into the sky. Chris thought it odd that the highly territorial creature seemed more or less unconcerned about the presence of Steel Samurai. Still, Chris was sure that once he attacked the monster that he would have its full attention. Ogre was at the apex of his jump when Steel Samurai's sword connected with the small monster. The effect was like a major league baseball player hitting a slow pitch softball, and Ogre was sent rocketing back into the desert.

Chris turned Steel Samurai in the direction of Yokozuna and began flying at roughly half of the mech's top speed. Chris had traveled over five kilometers before he looked at his radar screen to see that Ogre was not pursuing him but rather returning to attack the giant scorpion at the warehouse. Chris was slightly perplexed by Ogre's choice to attack the scorpion instead of Steel Samurai.

The pilot turned the robot around. "Okay, Ogre. I guess that I am just going to have to piss you off a little bit more to get your attention."

Kate and Dinah had run out into the street expecting to see the mech fighting off the scorpion and trying to save them. Their hearts sank when they saw the mech streaking out to meet the quickly approaching Ogre. Kate was watching as the mech hit Ogre with its sword until she heard Dinah scream. Kate's head whipped around to see the giant scorpion crawl around the corner of the burning warehouse. The creature looked at the two women for a brief second and then it charged them. Kate pushed Dinah to the ground and then she rolled under the scorpion's pincers as it reached down to grab her. The pincer came so close to Kate that she could actually feel the rough shell of the monster on her body as the bottom part of the pincer ran across her legs in mid roll.

Kate stood to see Dinah running down the street with the scorpion quickly closing in on her. Kate ran back into the warehouse and grabbed the burning torch that she had used to ignite the firewall. A torch was feeble protection against a thirty meter tall scorpion but it was all that she had to try and protect herself and save her friend with. She was sprinting after the monster, when out of the corner of her eye, she saw Ogre leaping toward the scorpion. She was glad to see the wretched beast because she at least knew that he would save Dinah from the scorpion. Kate's thoughts of Ogre saving Dinah were quickly dashed to pieces when she saw the mech come flying in to swat Ogre to ground once again before quickly turning and flying in the opposite direction.

Kate screamed, "Noooo!" when she saw the scorpion reach out and slice Dinah in half with its pincers. The giant creature quickly scooped up the remains of Dinah, and then it devoured them. Kate fell to her knees and began crying as she looked toward the fleeing mech. She did not know why the mech was using a hit and run attack on Ogre instead of standing and fighting him. All that she did know was that if the mech pilot had not attacked Ogre and run that either he would have seen her and Dinah, or Ogre would have at least attacked the scorpion and Dinah would still be alive.

Kate's thoughts quickly changed from Dinah to herself when she saw the scorpion turn around and start moving in her direction.

Chris checked his radar to once more find Ogre jumping in the direction of the giant scorpion instead of chasing Steel Samurai. Chris turned the mech around again, and this time he armed Steel Samurai's weapons systems.

Kate was running with the scorpion closing in on her with each step she took. She turned to see the scorpion's pincer swiping toward her, and she threw herself to the ground and pressed her nearly naked body against the scorching hot parking lot blacktop. The pincer slashed the air over her face, and she held the torch up to the hard shell of the monster. She watched as her feeble torch was blown out by the displaced air from the movement of the scorpion's pincer, as if it were a mere matchstick. Kate began rolling her body across the concrete cutting and bruising herself in a feeble attempt to put more distance between herself and the giant scorpion. She had rolled over roughly six parking spots before the monster was looming over her again. When the shadow of the creature fell upon her, Kate began to cry. It was at that moment, that she saw the dark form of Ogre falling from the sky. Ogre landed directly on top of the scorpion's face, driving it into the blacktop.

Kate stood as Ogre delivered a series of brutal punches to the scorpion's face that forced the monster to back up. Kate turned her head to see the mech streaking back toward the warehouse. She quickly decided that her only hope of survival would be to gain the attention of the pilot inside of the mech. Kate grabbed her still smoldering burnt chair leg and sprinted back to the remains of the firewall. She turned the corner to discover that the fire had spread from her makeshift wall to the warehouse itself. The sight of the burning warehouse doubled Kate's resolve. She knew that without the warehouse that she would dead within the next twenty-four hours.

She relit her torch from the burning warehouse, and then ran back into the parking lot to see the scorpion use its claw to knock Ogre into the burning building. Kate ran across the parking lot waving the torch overhead in hopes that she could attract the attention of the mech pilot.

Chris watched as the scorpion swiped his pincer at Ogre and knocked the beast into the inferno. From the information that he had on Ogre, he was pretty sure that the fire would do little more than piss him off. Chris had decided that for whatever reason Ogre was more concerned with the giant scorpion than he was with Steel Samurai. Chris turned on his high powered machine gun and was targeting the distracting scorpion when he saw a woman running across the parking lot waving a torch over her head. Chris's hand dropped from the gun controls. He could hardly believe what he was seeing. A living human who had survived outside of the settlement. From the corner of his eye, Chris saw Ogre jump out of the fire to attack the scorpion again. The monster began savagely beating on the scorpion while Chris carefully landed Steel Samurai near the woman.

The mech had no sooner set foot on the ground than Kate was using the last of her strength to scale the long ladder up to the entrance of the robot. Kate heard a roar and looked to her left to see Ogre trapped in the scorpion's pincer and screaming in pain. Kate secretly hoped that the scorpion would kill Ogre, but deep in her heart, she knew that the giant mutant didn't stand a chance in this battle.

The hatch above her opened and a young man reached down, grabbed her, and pulled her inside of the mech.

Kate was lying on the floor bleeding and nearly naked. She looked over at the pilot. "Kill him! Kill Ogre now!"

The pilot shook his head. "I'm sorry. I couldn't kill him even if I wanted to. He is too powerful. I need him to follow me to something else that will kill him. That is, of course, if he survives his battle with that scorpion."

Kate looked out of the mech's eyes to see Ogre snap the pincer in two that was wrapped around him. Kate shrugged. "That scorpion won't last another minute. Take off at top speed. Wherever you are going Ogre will find you."

The pilot was back at the controls of the mech when he looked over his shoulder at Kate. "How do you know that he will find us?"

Kate began to cry. "He will find us because you have me."

The pilot could tell from the look on Kate's face that she truly believed that Ogre would find them. The mech rocketed across the desert sky at full speed as the pilot walked over to Kate and helped her off of the floor. "I'm Chris Myers." The pilot waved his hand around the interior of the mech. "The mech has the code name *Steel Samurai*."

Kate sat up slowly. "I'm Kate Summers. Thank you for saving my life."

Ogre fell to the ground, and then he tossed away the remains of the scorpion's pincer. He then leapt on the back of the scorpion, punched through its shell, and used his hand to tear a large opening in the mutant's armor. Ogre began clawing and tearing at the soft tissue beneath the scorpion's shell. Ogre gouged out a huge chunk of flesh from the mutant, tossed it aside, and then climbed into the body of the scorpion itself. The scorpion spun in a frantic circle as Ogre tore it apart from the inside. The scorpion spun for five complete circles before Ogre had caused too much damage to its body. The scorpion slowly slumped to the ground and died.

With his foe vanquished, Ogre climbed out of the opening that he had created. Ogre roared at the dead mutant, and then he looked in the direction that Steel Samurai had flown. The mech was out of sight but Ogre could still smell his pet. Ogre snarled, and then leapt into the air in pursuit of his pet.

CHAPTER 13

Outside of Santa Fe

Chris brought some bread, water, and fruit to Kate. She ate the food with almost a reverence for it. It was the first time in three years that she had eaten something that wasn't partially cooked beef or bison.

After she was done eating she began asking Chris the dozens of questions that were swirling in her mind, "Thank God you finally came for us. Did the mechs fight off the other kaiju? Where is the government currently located? What kind of trap are you leading Ogre into? Will there be other mech's ready to help you kill him?"

Chris put his hands up. "Okay, slow down. I'll answer all of your questions but first tell me how long Ogre has held you captive. That will give me a good idea about where to start filling you in at."

Kate almost broke down in tears as the words left her mouth, "That monster had me and several other women held captive for three years." She was silent for a moment. "The others are all dead. I am the last one of Ogre's captives that is still alive." She began to cry, but then she quickly composed herself. "The last thing that I remember before Ogre captured us was Giladon attacking. Shortly after that, Ogre grabbed me." She took another deep breath as she continued to fight back her tears. "It was horrible living with that monster. He kept us like pets trapped in his warehouse. He fed us bison that he killed. Thankfully we had running water. That monster would just lay around and stare at us for hours on end. One of the girls tried to escape, and Ogre killed her for attempting to leave. Later, another group did escape. They were gone for several days, but Ogre eventually tracked them down and brought them back. He killed most of them too."

Kate's voice suddenly took on a much more positive tone, "That's all over now, though. You are going to lead Ogre into a trap and kill him. Then you can take me back to civilization—take me somewhere safe from monsters and mutants."

Chris tried to sound as consoling as possible, "There is no civilization. There is nowhere that is safe. The kaiju rule North America. They crushed both the military and the mechs. Steel Samurai is the last of the mechs." Chris took a deep breath. "We don't have any contact with the rest of the world. As far as we know the kaiju have destroyed the rest of humanity as well."

Chris gave Kate a second to let what he had said to her sink in, and then he continued, "There is a settlement in Kansas where several thousand people are living. Again, as far as we know, the settlement is the last living population of humans on Earth."

Kate's face became filled with fear and sadness. Chris knew exactly what she was thinking. Facing one's own death was one thing but realizing that your species was on the verge of extinction was an overwhelming thought. Chris hung his head slightly as he explained his quest to her, "Steel Samurai and I were the protectors of the settlement. I fought off attacks from several mutants but with each attack we lost more people and resources. Several days ago it looked as though our water supply might have become contaminated with radiation."

Chris stood and turned away from Kate as he continued to explain his actions. His guilt over leaving the settlement was still tearing him up inside, and he did not feel that he could look another person in the eyes as he told her about abandoning everyone. "It became clear to me that I was only postponing the inevitable. Every battle I fought only delayed the death of every member of the settlement and of the human race." Chris's guilt over leaving the people of the settlement finally overwhelmed him, and he broke down crying. "I knew that I had to do something drastic. I knew that in order for humanity to survive that we needed to destroy all of the monsters. Steel Samurai could kill a few giant bugs or rodents, but there was no way that he could destroy the True Kaiju, like Ogre, or Atomic Rex." Chris fell to his knees. "So I took the only option that I had available to me. I climbed into Steel Samurai and left the settlement. I left the last surviving members of the human race unprotected so that I could draw the True Kaiju into each other's territory. I knew that Steel Samurai could not defeat them, but I thought that they might be able to kill each other. I drew the Colony out of Los Angeles and right into Amebos where that thing absorbed every last giant ant. Then I had Yokozuna chase me into Giladon's territory. The giant killed the monster, and the last time that I saw him he was eating the remains of Giladon. Next, I was hoping to get Ogre to attack Yokozuna so that one of them could kill the other."

Chris started screaming, "This whole thing could be in vain though! A giant centipede could already have killed everyone in the settlement. I could very well have left them all to die while trying to enact a plan that I know is likely to fail."

Kate crawled over to Chris, and she hugged him. She was crying too as she spoke into his ear, "You had to make a decision that no one else in the history of the human race has had to make. You looked at everything that was going on around you and you chose to take the only course of action that you could." She turned his face so that he was looking her in the eyes. "You are a brave man and a hero. You have already saved my life, and you are doing all that you can to save the human race entirely on your own."

Chris hugged Kate as hard as he could. He had just met this woman, but she had told him exactly what he needed to hear. Having another human being condone his actions gave Chris a sense of both peace and renewed confidence.

Kate hugged him back. "You don't have to do this alone anymore. I can help you." Kate's quick thinking mind immediately began focusing on how she could help Chris. Foremost on her mind, was how to kill the horrid Ogre. She knew that her former jailer was pursuing them at this very moment. She took a look around the mech and an idea began to form. She gestured to the stairs leading to the floor below the cockpit. "It's been a while since I saw the report on the mechs, but if I remember correctly, there are living quarters below the cockpit. Do you have a sink or a shower down there?"

"We have both."

Kate nodded. "The shower in particular, does the water get recycled or is it dumped outside of the mech somehow?"

"The water from the shower is dumped outside of Steel Samurai when it's over a secure location. The shower is mainly a precaution for radiation removal due the monsters and Steel Samurai's radioactive core."

Kate ran her hand across Chris's face. "You are pretty cleanly shaven, do you have a razor that I could borrow?"

Chris nodded as he looked at Kate's nearly naked and hair covered body. "Yes, it's in the shower."

Kate smiled. 'Then I think I can clean myself up a little so I that can I feel something like a human and at the same time help draw Ogre into a battle with Yokozuna."

Kate stood and walked toward the stairs. Chris called after her, "I have a few extra clothes. They might be a bit big on you, but I will put them outside of the shower."

Kate thanked him, and then headed down the stairs. Chris briefly returned to the cockpit. He looked out of Steel Samurai as the desert and sky flew past him. Finding Kate, saving her, talking to her, having her comfort him and validate his mission had lifted a huge burden off his shoulders. For the first time in years, Chris had a sense of hope.

CHAPTER 14

As the warm water poured over her body Kate was overwhelmed with a sense of pleasure that she never thought that she would experience again. The world was full of monsters and mutants, and after going nearly three years without being able to shave her legs or armpits, Kate almost felt like a werewolf. Before the giant monsters had taken over the world, Kate had enjoyed watching post-apocalyptic television shows like *The Walking Dead*. While she enjoyed the show she always thought that it was funny how cleaned up the female actresses were. In a world where people had to struggle to find food and water, the women of *The Walking Dead* always were always squeaky clean, had shaved legs, and plucked eyebrows. The show was obviously going for ratings over realism. When fanboys want to watch a comic on TV they wanted to see hot chicks, not what post-apocalyptic woman would really look like.

Kate scraped another long line of hair off her leg. In addition to the hair, there was also a good deal of dead skin and blood from her various wounds going down the drain. While the entire process made Kate physically and emotionally feel better, it was also serving a functional purpose. Kate was pretty sure that Ogre could track her and the other woman through his sense of smell. All of Kate's hair, skin, and blood was swirling around in the tank below the shower. When Kate was done showering Chris would fly Steel Samurai directly over Yokozuna where he was going to empty the shower's waste water directly on top of the giant. With all of Kate's genetic material mixed in with the water, the hope was that it would draw Ogre right to Yokozuna. A long thin strip of dead skin peeled off Kate's leg, and she smiled as she thought about Yokozuna crushing Ogre to death.

When she finished her shower she climbed out and looked at herself in the mirror. She was pleased with the improvement. She took a hard look at the jumbled mess on top of her head and realized that her hair still needed work. The fact that it had been three years since she had a haircut still gave her head the look of a cave woman. Being a military man, Chris had an electric pair of clippers on hand as well that he used to keep his hair cut short. Kate was not able to do much with the clippers, but she was able to shorten her hair to the point of no longer being a tangled mess.

When she was done cleaning herself she slipped on Chris's extra flight suit. The suit was baggy on her and long, but the psychological relief of no longer being nearly naked was huge for Kate. After running around with her body fully exposed for two years, the flight suit looked like a prom dress to the young woman.

She cleaned up the meager washroom, and then she headed back up the stairs to the cockpit where Chris was staring at the radar screen. Kate could see several large blips that kept coming across the screen. She walked up next to Chris. "Is that thing on the radar, Ogre?"

Chris shook his head. "No. We lost Ogre a while back. That target is in front of us. It's Yokozuna. He is exactly where I left him. He's probably still feeding on what's left of Giladon."

Kate pointed to the other blips that kept popping up at the top of the screen above Yokozuna. "What are those blips that keep coming and going?"

Chris sighed. "They could be a problem. Giladon's been dead for over twenty-four hours. Those other things are scavengers flying around the kill. Given that they are coming up on radar I think that we can assume that they are giant mutants of some kind."

"What do you think that they are?"

Chris shrugged. "My best guess would be buzzards, but we will find out when we get there. I have slowed down our speed some to make sure that we don't get to Yokozuna to far ahead of Ogre." Chris finally turned to Kate, and his breath was almost taken away. She was a strikingly beautiful woman. She was nearly nude when Chris had first met her, but he was not in the mindset to look at her as a woman. Like an emergency rescue worker, Chris was focused on saving the woman, not on her appearance. Now that he had a brief moment of calm, Chris was seeing Kate as a woman for the first time.

Kate noticed him staring at her, and he quickly asked her about the bait that they had set for Ogre, "I see you cut your hair? Do you think that you put enough genetic material in the shower drainage system to attract Ogre?"

Kate smiled. "There has to be almost a pound of blood, hair, and skin from me in the system. I've seen Ogre track a car full of women across the desert after they had over a twenty-four hour head start. If he tracks us by smell then it should be more than enough to draw him to Yokozuna." Kate's voice took on a dark tone, "I hope that Yokozuna crushes that freak."

Chris nodded in reply. He still hated Yokozuna, and he had hoped that Ogre would kill the obese giant, but his hatred was different from Kate's hatred. Chris hated Yokozuna for what he represented but Kate hated Ogre for what he had done to her.

Kate was looking out of Steel Samurai's eye shields when she saw a large hill up ahead of them. She gasped when she saw the hill move. The hill rolled over to show the bloated face of a horrifying giant. Yokozuna was rolling around in a large pile of blood and bones. All that remained of Giladon was his horn, his club like tail, a few bones, and a pool of blood. When Yokozuna rolled dozens of black shapes each about the size of a city bus flew into the air. When the shapes jumped into the air Kate could make out that they were giant mutant flies. Kate thought that the flies were the most disgusting thing that she would ever see until Yokozuna grabbed one of the giant insects and shoved into his mouth.

Kate had to choke back a mouthful of vomit. Her struggle to keep from vomiting was not helped as Chris suddenly increased the speed of Steel Samurai. She had to grab onto Chris's pilot seat to keep from falling over.

Chris yelled, "Hold on, I am going to fly low and quick over Yokozuna while he is laying down. It will give us a chance to make the drop without having to worry about him attacking us."

When Yokozuna saw Steel Samurai flying toward him the giant started to sit up. He recognized the metal monster that had attacked him before and he was angry to see it again. Before Yokozuna could stand, Steel Samurai streaked over him. The corpulent giant did not even notice the tank full of water that the robot had dropped on him. Yokozuna watched Steel Samurai fly over him and into the distance. With the mech gone, the giant sat back down, picked up one of the remaining bones of Giladon, and began chewing on it.

Steel Samurai was several miles away from Yokozuna when Chris finally landed the mech.

Kate moved up next to Chris. "What do we do now?"

Chris pointed at the radar. "We watch the radar. When another blip comes onto it that looks like Ogre we fly back to Yokozuna. Then we hover at a safe distance and wait for Ogre. When he shows up we just watch them fight until one of them kills the other."

Kate nodded hoping that Ogre would be the monster who died today, because if he did not, she was sure that the beast would continue pursuing her.

Ogre crashed into the desert sand after completing a leap of nearly five kilometers. The monster lifted his head into the air and sniffed. He had been following the faint trail of his captive ever since the metal man had taken her away, but suddenly the smell increased in its intensity. What was more, Ogre could now tell that his former captive was no longer moving. Ogre growled knowing that Kate was no longer inside of the metal man and that she had stopped moving. Ogre looked in the direction of Kate's scent, and then he leapt into the sky after it.

Chris and Kate sat in silent and eager anticipation for nearly an hour until a blip appeared at the bottom of Chris's radar screen, and then disappeared. A moment later the blip reappeared again, this time closer to Yokozuna before dropping out. Chris slammed his hands into the control panel in excitement. "It's coming and going because the object is leaping into the air and then dropping back down as it makes it way to Yokozuna."

Kate gritted her teeth. "It's Ogre."

Chris didn't waste time answering her. He simply hit Steel Samurai's ignition button and flew toward the forthcoming battle.

Several minutes later Steel Samurai was hovering above Yokozuna as the giant tried to catch another fly to stuff into his mouth. Yokozuna reached up for a fly but he stopped short of grabbing it and stood perfectly still as he looked south of his current position. The giant grunted, and then began walking in a southwest direction.

Chris kept his eyes fixed on Yokozuna as he talked to Kate, "He senses Ogre approaching. The kaiju are very territorial. Since he killed Giladon, Yokozuna now sees this area as part of his territory. Yokozuna will instinctively attack Ogre in an attempt to drive him out of his territory or kill him."

Steel Samurai slowly drifted after Yokozuna until he saw a pitch black object standing out against the blue sky that was roughly eye level with the mech's current altitude.

Kate shuddered when she saw Ogre attain the height of the robot. She put her hand on Chris's shoulder. "Can you take us a little higher?"

Chris nodded. "Good idea." He then took Steel Samurai up another one hundred meters.

Ogre could smell Kate's scent growing stronger, and when he saw the large form of Yokozuna ahead of him, Ogre was able to identify her smell on the giant. Ogre was unsure if Yokozuna was holding Kate captive or if he had devoured her. Either way, Ogre was furious. Ogre crashed into the ground, and despite the fact that Yokozuna was nearly ten times larger than he was, the monster roared a challenge at the giant.

Yokozuna bellowed a challenge in return at the beast that had invaded his territory, and then he charged at Ogre.

Ogre leapt into the air and slammed into Yokozuna's stomach with the force of a small earthquake. Waves of blubber went cascading across the giant's stomach, but Yokozuna was otherwise unaffected by the blow. Ogre's fist was still wedged in Yokozuna's gut when the giant used his hand to swat Ogre off of him. Ogre slammed into the ground below him. He rolled over onto his back to see Yokozuna's large foot coming down at him. Ogre quickly stood and placed his hands above his head, catching Yokozuna's foot, and stopping it from descending any farther. The ground beneath Ogre began to crack under the pressure, but the monster held Yokozuna's enormous foot at bay. Then in a display of incredible strength, Ogre heaved and threw Yokozuna's foot into the air—causing the giant to lose his balance and fall onto his back.

Chris shook his head in disbelief. "Yokozuna weighs as much as a mountain. I can't believe that Ogre was able to toss him like that. How strong is he?"

Kate kept her eyes fixed on the monsters. "I have seen him do things that you wouldn't believe. He is the strongest creature walking the face of the Earth."

Ogre ran forward and grabbed Yokozuna's toe with his arms. Then he twisted the pudgy digit and snapped it in half. Yokozuna moaned in pain, and then he used his other foot to kick Ogre, sending the smaller monster tumbling through the desert.

Ogre was tumbling head over heels until he dug his hands into the dirt. He skidded several meters before coming to a stop. Ogre growled and then leapt back at Yokozuna. The giant was just starting to sit up when Ogre crashed into his face. The force of the blow sent Yokozuna's head crashing back into the desert floor. Ogre dug his left hand into Yokozuna's nostril, and then he brought his right hand crashing into the giant's nose.

There was a loud snap that Chris and Kate could hear inside of Steel Samurai as Yokozuna's nose was shattered. Blood's poured out of Yokozuna's nostrils as he reached up and wrapped his fat hand around Ogre. This time Yokozuna tossed Ogre across the desert. Ogre flew out of the sight of Chris and Kate before he landed head first in the desert and created a large chasm across the sand as he slid to a stop. Ogre pulled himself out of the sand, growled, and then leapt again in the direction of Yokozuna.

Yokozuna slowly stood on his broken toe. When the blood oozed down to his mouth the ravenous giant licked it up. He was staggering in the direction that he had thrown his opponent when he saw the pitch black form of Ogre leaping back toward him. Ogre landed several hundred meters from the giant, and then he leapt at a low angle that sent his body hurtling into Yokozuna's knee. The impact shifted Yokozuna's knee cap to the side, and the giant roared in anguish before falling onto his side. When Yokozuna crashed into the desert he was eye level with Ogre, who bore his long fangs and roared at the fallen giant. Yokozuna's hand shot out with a speed that Ogre was unprepared for. In the blink of an eye, Yokozuna had grabbed Ogre and stuffed the monster into his mouth.

Kate saw Yokozuna jam Ogre into his mouth and she let out a sigh of relief. "Thank God, Ogre is finally dead."

Chris kept his eyes fixed on Yokozuna. "I don't think that this fight is over yet."

Kate took a closer look at Yokozuna and gasped when she saw that the giant's mouth was still open. Yokozuna was trying as hard as he could to bite down, but Ogre had his hands placed on the giant's upper jaw and his feet pressed against his tongue. Ogre's entire body was shaking, but he was slowly forcing Yokozuna's mouth open.

Blood began to pour out of Yokozuna's mouth as his jaw was stretched beyond its limits. Ogre continued to force Yokozuna's jaws to open wider and there was another sickening *crack* when the giant's lower jaw reached its limit and snapped off.

Ogre fell to the ground while Yokozuna's lower jaw hung from his face like a shattered piñata. The giant fell onto his backside. He then made a vain effort to push his jaw back into place. Yokozuna had his hands on his jaw when Ogre leapt up again and threw his body into Yokozuna's face. The force of the blow once more sent Yokozuna sprawling onto his back. Ogre hand landed on the giant's stomach, which he crawled across as he made his way to Yokozuna's face. Yokozuna was still trying to push his jaw back into place when Ogre climbed onto his forehead and delivered an earth shattering blow. The monster repeatedly punched the giant in the forehead with enough force to shatter a skyscraper.

Chris and Kate watched in horror when Yokozuna's hands fell to his side and what was left of his face slowly started to sink in on itself as Ogre continued to pound on it. A few moments later Yokozuna's face was reduced to a mound of blood and flesh after Ogre had crushed the entire front half of his skull.

Chris was still staring at the carnage as he whispered, "Rot in hell, you fat bastard."

Ogre looked down at the remains of his opponent and roared at the slain giant. Ogre then sniffed the air and looked up at Steel Samurai. Kate dug her hands into Chris's shoulder, and shouted, "He knows that I am in the robot! Quick, get us out of here."

Chris was trying to calm her down when he saw Ogre leap at Steel Samurai. Even with the mech's increased altitude the monster had just missed the robot's foot. Chris rose another hundred meters, and then he shot off in an eastward direction at supersonic speed.

Ogre watched the mech fly away. Then he roared and leapt after it.

CHAPTER 15

Atlantic Ocean

Atomic Rex moved gracefully through the warm waters of the Atlantic Ocean. The salty water felt soothing to the kaiju as it passed over his scales. The kaiju's aggressive nature caused him to have many painful experiences, as such, the pleasurable sensation of swimming in the ocean was not lost on Atomic Rex.

He was on the outskirts of what he considered to be his oceanic territory. The kaiju's aquatic domain covered from the northern tip of what was once Maryland to the Hudson Bay. After defeating the giant crabs, Atomic Rex had rested for a day before heading back to water, swimming to the edge of his territory, and then swimming north. The monster was searching for any further incursions into his domain. When he had swam back to the waters off the coast of New Jersey, the mutated dinosaur cracked open the shell of the crab that he had left blind and limbless. Atomic Rex then devoured the disabled beast and ended its tortured existence.

The kaiju had returned to the surface to take a breath of air and watched as the leviathan that he had sensed nearby surfaced as well. The enormous creature was at least three times the size of Atomic Rex himself. The creature had once been a blue whale until the radiation given off by the kaiju had turned it into a creature of incredible size.

Atomic Rex would typically regarded a creature that was as large or larger than himself to be a threat to his territory, but the kaiju had seen other mutated whales in his waters. The creatures were huge but harmless. They simply swam through Atomic Rex's domain without trying to take anything from his food supply or to challenge his rule. Atomic Rex was not a berserk killing machine. If a creature was not a threat to him or food he would leave it in relative peace. Being aware of the benign nature of the whale, Atomic Rex was content to let the gentle giant pass through his domain unimpeded. Atomic Rex was currently swimming slightly behind the mutant whale and coasting along in his wake.

Atomic Rex swam alongside the enlarged whale until the two mutants were nearing the Hudson Bay. Atomic Rex was preparing to leave the monster and turn back toward land when his senses detected the presence of another larger predator lurking in the nearby waters. The kaiju came to a stop and focused on the vibrations in the water near him. Based on the way that the predator was moving, Atomic Rex could sense that the creature was hunting the whale and not him. Despite the fact that the predator was not hunting him, it was clearly aware that Atomic Rex was nearby. Since he was close to the edge of his territory, Atomic Rex was content to let the mutant whale swim out of his waters. Once the whale had left his waters Atomic Rex would be unconcerned with the whale or the predator. Atomic Rex was about to start swimming into the Hudson Bay when he sensed the predator dart toward the whale. Atomic Rex snarled in anger. Had the predator waited a few minutes more to attack it would have been clear of Atomic Rex's domain, but the creature had opted to enter his territory. An incursion into his territory by another large predator was something that Atomic Rex could not abide. The mutated dinosaur quickly surfaced, filled his lungs with fresh air, and then began swimming at full speed toward the charging predator.

Atomic Rex was streaking through the water when he was finally able to see the predator. The beast was a mutant like himself. In this case, the mutant was a female great white shark that had been enlarged to a size equal to that of Atomic Rex. The shark was aware of the approaching kaiju, but her hunger outweighed her caution. The shark ignored the threat of Atomic Rex as she continued to swim toward the whale. The shark had almost reached the whale when Atomic Rex slammed into her side and pushed her off course. Atomic Rex wrapped his arms around the shark and dug into her body with his long claws. He had opened his mouth when in an unbelievable flash of speed and flexibility the shark's head swung around and bit into the kaiju's shoulder. The shark's teeth sliced through Atomic Rex tough hide as if were made of paper. The kaiju pulled his shoulders free of the shark's jaws, but he lost a large chunk of flesh in the process. Atomic Rex glared at the shark, and then he attacked her.

The two apex predators rolled in the ocean depths as they tried to tear each other apart.. Blood from the two creatures seeped out into the water. The blood not only attracted other smaller predators, but when they ate it, the blood began to slowly mutate them as well. The sea life that was now feeding off of the blood of a kaiju would one day soon become kaiju themselves.

While the smaller creatures fed off the carnage the two monsters continued to tear each other to shreds. Realizing that he was receiving as much damage as he was giving, Atomic Rex used his powerful arms to push the mutant shark off him.

At first the shark swam away from Atomic Rex, but after swimming a short distance, she turned around. The kaiju watched as the shark circled him. The simple minded shark had long since forgotten about the defenseless whale. To the shark, Atomic Rex had now become her prey. The shark dove at Atomic Rex, aiming to attack the kaiju's throat.

Seeing the shark coming for him, Atomic Rex attempted to swim upward to avoid the attack, but in its element the shark was far quicker than the mutated dinosaur. Atomic Rex had moved enough to keep the shark from attacking his throat, but the kaiju's leg was still within the shark's reach. The shark's jaws shot forward from her mouth and tore into Atomic Rex's calf. Atomic Rex grunted in pain, but he fought back the urge to roar knowing that doing so would expel his remaining oxygen.

Blood poured out of Atomic Rex's leg and pain shot through his body, but this only served to anger the powerful beast. Atomic Rex swung his head down and bit into the shark's tail fin. With one pull, the kaiju tore the appendage off, causing the shark to release her grip. The shark tried in vain to swim away, but without its tail fin, the once feared predator sank slowly to the ocean floor.

Seeing that his opponent was mortally wounded Atomic Rex moved in for the kill. The kaiju swam up behind the injured shark and bit into her pectoral fin. The shark writhed in pain as she tried to swing her head around to bite the kaiju, but Atomic Rex had gauged the shark's abilities during their battle. The kaiju was well aware of how far the shark's mouth could reach, and he had made sure that he was out of the shark's bite range. Atomic Rex bit off the shark's pectoral fin, and then he proceeded to tear into her spine. Several minutes later the shark finally perished. Atomic Rex released the dead shark, and then swam to the surface of the ocean. When he broke the waves he roared in triumph, and then refilled his lung with precious air.

The kaiju looked toward the Hudson Bay and land. His awesome atomic abilities were already working to repair his damaged leg. Despite the damage done to it, his body would fully heal the wound within a day or two. Atomic Rex needed to rest, and in order to do so, he would need to reach land. The kaiju was satisfied that he fought off any threats to his aquatic domain. Now he would swim to land and rest before starting the long trek across the large area of land that was also his in search of threats and food. The kaiju swam to shore, strode out of the water and laid down on the banks of the bay. The mighty Atomic Rex then closed his eyes and fell asleep as his incredible body continued to heal his injured leg.

CHAPTER 16

Steel Samurai was flying over the mid-west as it headed for its next target. Inside the robot, Chris was beyond ecstatic. The Colony, Giladon, and Yokozuna were all dead. Not only was the direct threat that they represented gone, but so too was the threat of walking around and giving birth to lesser mutants as a result of their ambient radiation. Chris smiled and shook his head as he thought to himself that his plan was working. He had doubts about his plan, but now that it was over a third of the way complete, he was starting to believe that he could pull it off.

Chris went over to his computer and took a deep breath as he typed the name *Atomic Rex* into his keyboard. The next part of his plan would call for him to face arguably the most powerful of all of the kaiju and the creature that had killed his friends and sent him running in mankind's last stand against the monsters. Chris was reviewing the information on the monster that had already been ingrained in his head when they had last battled. He read the bio on the monster aloud, "Atomic Rex: Fifty meters tall, sixty-five meters long. The kaiju is extremely physically powerful and highly resistant to physical injury. Atomic Rex also appears to have an advanced healing ability that allows him to recover from his injuries at an accelerated rate. The monster is highly radioactive. He possesses the ability to let out a short range nuclear burst in the form of his Atomic Wave attack. Atomic Rex has claimed most of the North Eastern United States as his territory." Chris nodded at the screen. "All right, big boy, it's time for you to venture out into new lands." Chris called out, "Kate, come on over here so I can show you what's next." Chris looked behind him, but he was unable find Kate. He called out to her again, and when she didn't answer, he started searching the interior of Steel Samurai for her.

Kate was sitting in the shower with her arms wrapped around her legs and her face buried in her knees. She had the water pressure turned on full blast and the water as hot as she could withstand. Tears streamed down her face as the fear crept back into her mind that this could be the last time that she experienced the safety that she thought she had found. She had been strong for Chris and for herself when she was first rescued, but all of that strength seeped out of her body when she saw Ogre kill Yokozuna. Yokozuna was the largest thing that Kate had ever beheld, and Ogre crushed the giant as if he were a frail child. Kate continued to cry when she heard a knock on the door. She didn't answer Chris; she simply buried her face deeper into her legs and continued to cry.

Chris knocked on the door again. "Kate, are you okay?" When she didn't answer, Chris opened the door and walked into the steam filled room. He walked in the direction of the shower where he found Kate balled up and crying. He didn't know what specifically was bothering her, but he knew how she felt and what she needed from him. When Chris's emotions had overwhelmed him and he broke down, Kate held him and comforted him. He didn't even bother to turn off the water; he simply climbed into the warm shower, knelt, and held her.

Chris didn't say anything to Kate. He just held her, and a few minutes later she finally opened up, "This isn't going to last. I am never going to be safe for the rest of my life. Ogre will track me down no matter where I go. He beat that giant to death with his bare hands. Even Steel Samurai won't be able to stop him."

She looked at Chris. "When he finds us he will kill you, and hopefully, me too. I don't want to die, but I would prefer death to being his pet again." She wrapped her arms around Chris. "Just leave me somewhere, Chris. Why should both of us die? Just give him what he wants and maybe he will let you live." Kate was nearly panting with fear. "If he doesn't kill me for running away then I will anger him to the point of ending my existence. At least then, I will finally be free of that monster."

Chris hugged Kate as tight as he could. "No, Kate. I could never leave you." He put his hand under her chin. "Ogre can be killed. Not by me or Steel Samurai, but if we stick to the plan that monster will meet his match. After Ogre captured you, there were several other monsters that appeared. One of them was called

Atomic Rex. Steel Samurai and I tried to battle him along with two other mech pilots. He destroyed the other two mechs in less than five minutes. Atomic Rex is thought to be the most powerful of all of the kaiju." Chris took a deep breath. "We are going to put that to the test by drawing Atomic Rex into conflict with another powerful kaiju known as *Dimetrasaurs.* If Ogre is still following us we will lead him into a battle with the winner of that encounter."

Kate's body shuddered. "He'll destroy them too. I know it."

Chris smiled. "If he does there is still a giant acid spewing turtle and a wad of jelly the size of a city for him to contend with. He can hit Amebos as much as he wants. All that it will do is make that wad of goo jiggle."

Kate laughed a little, and then looked Chris in the eyes. She was still terrified that Ogre would find her, but at this moment, she was with Chris. Kate's emotions were overwhelming her, and she thought that even if she was only with Chris for another day that she was going to make the most of their time together. She reached over and kissed Chris. When he pulled in closer, instead of pushing her away, she began to unzip his soaking wet jump suit.

Chris had wanted to make love to Kate ever since she had comforted him several days ago. He wasn't sure how she felt about him, so out of respect, he kept his feelings to himself. Now that she made the first move Chris let his passion for her take over. Once his clothes were off, he gently laid her down in the shower as he continued to kiss her. As far as they knew they were last two people on the face of the Earth, and they made love to each other as if they were.

When they had finished making love they turned off the shower and simply held onto each other for a while. Kate still feared that Ogre was going to find them, but Chris had given her a reason to hope that she could have a life after Ogre. An alarm went off throughout Steel Samurai. Kate looked to Chris. "What does that alarm mean?"

Chis slowly started to stand. "It means that we have crossed into Atomic Rex's territory. It's time we found the Lizard King and provoked him into chasing us."

CHAPTER 17

Chris flew Steel Samurai to the southern tip of Atomic Rex's territory. When they had reached the Chesapeake Bay Chris pointed out at the water as he addressed Kate, "We will start here and work our way north. Finding Atomic Rex could be difficult. His territory covers everything on land from Maryland to New York, and he seems to regularly swim as far as forty kilometers out to sea along that same stretch of land." He turned to Kate. "We have a lot of area to cover. I don't think that flying over the ocean looking for Atomic Rex is going to be overly productive. Even with Steel Samurai's sonar capabilities, finding a moving target like him in the ocean would be difficult. I think that it would be best if we were to work a grid pattern across his land based territory, sooner or later we are bound to find him."

Kate nodded and hugged him. Chris then sent Steel Samurai flying north along the coast. Kate looked out the eyes of Steel Samurai and at the city of Baltimore. The area around the inner harbor had sustained heavy damage. As they were flying over the harbor, Kate gasped when she saw something that looked like a giant walrus lying dead among the ruins. The giant animal's insides were torn out, and its tail was missing.

Chris stared at the dead beast. "All of the kaiju are territorial, but Atomic Rex is probably the most aggressive of all of the monsters. The monster will kill anything that it perceives as the slightest threat to his territory." Chris held Kate's hand. "I doubt that the walrus is the last dead mutant that we will find as we look for Atomic Rex."

Steel Samurai continued to make its way north, and with each new city that they came across, the level of devastation they found increased exponentially. When they had reached Dover Delaware the entire downtown district of the city was nothing but rubble.

Kate shook her head, "Why did Atomic Rex attack the cities to the north with more ferocity than he did cities in the southern part of his domain?"

Chris looked away from Kate for a moment. "When Atomic Rex made landfall at Coney Island there were still some remnants of humanity that tried to fight back against the monster. The National Guard, the police forces of the larger cities, and in some cases, just local militias with hunting rifles. All that these efforts did was to enrage Atomic Rex. Whenever he encountered a show of force the kaiju would totally destroy anything in the nearby vicinity. After each battle, word of Atomic Rex's destructive nature and power began to spread. People eventually realized that trying to fight him would only result in their deaths. They began to simply evacuate and let him have the land that he wanted. That's why Baltimore only suffered damage in the battle between Atomic Rex and the Walrus. Dover's entire business district was destroyed."

Kate shook her head in disbelief. "Then what happened to New York when he landed on Coney Island?"

Chris didn't answer he simply shook his head as tears began to fill his eyes. Kate walked over and hugged him. He cried in her arms as they continued to fly north in search of the monster that had caused the devastation below them and killed millions of people.

A half an hour later, Steel Samurai flew over the beaches of North Jersey where they saw the body of a gigantic dead shark below them.

Kate looked out at the dead beast, and whispered, "Before the end of the world I was a big fan of Steve Alten's MEG books. The creature down there is exactly how I would have pictured his megalodons looking in real life, except not all torn up. If Atomic Rex is the creature that ripped that monster to pieces, then I can't even imagine how terrifying the creature is in person."

Chris remained silent as Steel Samurai turned to its left and headed toward the decimated remains of what was once New York City.

Kate gasped when saw that all five boroughs had been reduced to dust and rubble. She put her hand on Chris's shoulder. "I can't believe it. There is not a single building left standing. It actually looks like a nuclear bomb hit the city."

Chris just kept staring at the meager remains of the dead city. He whispered under his breath, "This is my fault."

Kate turned to him. "What did you say?"

Chris hung his head. "I said that this if my fault."

Kate shook her head. "This isn't your fault. You told me that Atomic Rex destroyed an entire fleet of Naval warships and two other mechs. How were you and your friends supposed to stop him?"

Chris clenched his fists. "This is not my fault because I didn't stop him. This is my fault because I pissed him off. Had we not attacked Atomic Rex, had we just evacuated the city, maybe he would not have laid utter waste to it. Maybe some of New York would still be standing and maybe countless lives could have been saved." He turned away from her. "The two best friends that I had died here. Their mechs, Iron Avenger and Bronze Warrior, are still rusting down there as a reminder of my mistakes."

Kate pulled his face toward her, and she kissed him. "You couldn't have known that Atomic Rex would have inflicted this level of destruction when he was angered, but now you do know. Let's not let your pain and all of those lives go to waste. Let's use that knowledge to anger him again, and then lead him straight into Dimetrasaurs's territory and have him kill that monster."

Kate hugged Chris. "Thank you for showing me this."

Chris gave her a puzzled look. "Why would you thank me for showing you this horror?"

Kate looked back over the devastation. "Because now that I have seen this, for the first time, I can truly believe that there is a creature that can kill Ogre." She looked toward Chris. "You have already saved me from his clutches, and now by sharing the most painful event in your life, you have freed me from the fear of his wrath." She gave Chris a long and passionate kiss that was only interrupted by the sound of Steel Samurai's radar registering a target. They walked over to the radar, and Chris's eye grew wide.

Kate was a little scared by the look on his face. "What is *that* blip?"

Chris looked to Kate. "It's Atomic Rex heading upriver on the Hudson. He is patrolling his territory. The latest information that we have puts the western border of his domain at the mouth of the

Hudson River. That will put us right up by the Eerie Canal and the Great Lakes."

Chris pulled out a map of the area. "He will be brushing right up against Dimetrasaurs's territory." He turned to Kate. "We won't need to attack him and then have him chase across three states. He is already heading in the direction that we want. All that we have to do is to stay behind him and then attack him near the mouth of the Hudson. From there, he will follow us into Dimetrasaurs's territory."

He quickly kissed Kate. "We can do this. We can use Atomic Rex to destroy Dimetrasaurs." He hugged her and walked over to the cockpit. "I need to take another inventory of Steel Samurai's remaining ammunition. If it is at all possible, we want to avoid taking on that monster in close quarters combat."

Kate turned away from Chris to let him complete his weapons check. She then turned her attention to the blip on the screen that either ensured mankind's destruction or represented its best hope of continuing to exist as a species.

Baltimore

Ogre's long leap took him right into what was once the inner harbor of the city of Baltimore. The monster walked around the remains of the giant walrus. Keeping track of his pet's scent when she was concealed inside of the metal giant was difficult, but Ogre was nearly certain that the robot had taken her this way. There was also another smell that caught Ogre's attention as he walked around the corpse of the behemoth. Ogre walked up to the walrus and inhaled deeply. The scent was strong and Ogre was immediately able to determine that it came from a powerful creature. Ogre snarled, it seemed as if he would have to slay some other beast as well as the metal giant. Ogre howled in anger and determination. He then leapt into the air with his thoughts focused on crushing the metal man and this other monster who would seek to keep him from his pet.

CHAPTER 18

New York State

In a little over a day, Atomic Rex's wounds from his battle with the giant shark had completely healed. The mutant dinosaur had woken to find that he was hungry for both meat and radiation. The monster knew that he could absorb the radiation that he required from the abandon nuclear reactors at the Indian Point Nuclear Power Plant. The plant was located directly on the banks of the Hudson River. Atomic Rex was several kilometers down river from the plant, but his body could already feel the radiation that was seeping out from the plant calling to his very cells. The kaiju dipped his head back into the water and moved his tail with increased vigor as he continued to propel himself to the structure that would replenish his awesome power.

Chris was reviewing maps of the Hudson River valley when he noticed that the radar was indicating that Atomic Rex was increasing his speed. The increase in speed was not significant enough to indicate that the monster was hunting something, but Chris was sure that the kaiju was purposely heading to a specific destination. Chris returned to his maps and noticed the India Point Nuclear Power Plant. Chris said the words aloud, "He's going to the power plant to recharge his body."

Kate walked up behind him with some bread, fruit, and water. "Atomic Rex is going to recharge his body with more nuclear energy? Shouldn't we stop him before he does that?"

Chris shook his head. "Having that monster at full power scares that hell out of me, but if we are going to draw him into a battle with Dimetrasaurs and we have a possible battle with Ogre looming we, may want him at full power." He turned to Kate. "Ideally we want Atomic Rex to kill as many other kaiju as possible and to deplete his power source in the process. After he has done our dirty work for us and he is weak and exhausted, is when we want to destroy him." Chris sighed. "In the meantime, were are going to need to let him absorb as much nuclear energy as possible, and then attack him when his power is at its peak." He smiled at Kate. "I only hope that we can live long enough to have a fully powered Atomic Rex chase us into the Great Lakes."

Atomic Rex crawled out of the river as he approached the power plant. His foot crashed down into the rocky bank of the Hudson and the impact tremor that it created traveled to the power plant itself. The power plant shook, and as it did so, it awakened the beast slumbering next to the nuclear silos. At one point in its life, the creature had been a black bear who lived in the woods near the Hudson River. The radiation given off by Atomic Rex during his trips up the Hudson to the power plant had mutated the fish in the river to the point where they had become highly radioactive. The fish in turn were eaten by the bear, who also absorbed the radiation. The radiation caused a painful change to occur in the bear. Over the course of several years the bear had lost all of its fur and had grown to nearly ten times its previous size. During the growth process, the beast's teeth and claws had grown at a disproportional rate, causing them to become long for the bear even with its increased size. The bear's skin had split and torn many times during its growth, causing the monster to have large areas of open wounds that extend to musculature all over its body. There were still a few people living in the area when the monstrous bear first showed up, and they had named the beast Ursa Major.

While all of these changes had been painful to Ursa Major it was the hunger that most tore at the creature's stomach. With Ursa Major's increased size came an increased appetite. The bear's ravenous hunger had driven it to devour nearly all of the remaining fish population of the Hudson River. When Ursa Major stood on his hind legs to see what had awoken him from his slumber, he set his eyes on Atomic Rex and saw food. Ursa Major roared at Atomic Rex, and then he charged the mutated dinosaur.

Atomic Rex responded in kind with a roar of his own. Much like his battle with the giant octopus, Atomic Rex knew that at the conclusion of his battle with Ursa Major that one of them would be victorious and that the other one would be food.

Inside the cockpit of Steel Samurai, Chris and Kate were just finishing up eating when another radar target appeared on their screen.

Kate peered over at the radar screen. "Is that other blip Dimetrasaurs?"

Chris kept his eyes fixed on the screen. "I doubt that Dimetrasaurs would venture into Atomic Rex's territory on his own. It's probably some other mutant that was unluckily enough to have crossed paths with Atomic Rex. Still, let's hurry up and see what's going on. We should be able to stay back and high up enough to avoid either one of them noticing us." Chris then jumped into the pilot's seat and pushed Steel Samurai forward, while Kate held onto the back of his chair.

A few minutes later they could see Atomic Rex standing in front of them and roaring at some other creature. Chris increased Steel Samurai's altitude so that they could see over Atomic Rex and it was then that they both saw the giant bear. Chris leaned back in his chair. "It looks like we are in for a show."

Ursa Major lumbered forward while Atomic Rex sprinted at the massive mammal. When the two monsters reached each other Ursa Major stood on his hind legs and wrapped his arms around Atomic Rex's neck and shoulders. The bear scratched at Atomic Rex's back but his claws were unable to penetrate the hard alligator like caprice on the mutated dinosaur's back.

Atomic Rex dug his claws into Ursa Major's side. There was a sickening pop when the reptile's claws pierced the bear's hide. The two monsters grappled as each monster tried to the throw the other to the ground. When Ursa Major was on its hind legs it was nearly equal to Atomic Rex in height, but Atomic Rex was still double the bear's weight and mass. Atomic Rex shifted his weight briefly to his right, and then he pulled Ursa Major to the left with all of his strength and weight behind him. The result of the maneuver was that Atomic Rex sent Ursa Major tumbling to the ground.

Ursa Major rolled a few times before it was able to regain its footing. Ursa Major was standing on all fours when Atomic Rex rammed his head at a full sprint into the bear's side. The blow again knocked the smaller mutant to the ground. Ursa Major was attempting to stand when Atomic Rex's thick tail swung around and crashed into the bear's face and shoulder once more, knocking it back to the ground. Ursa Major looked up to see Atomic Rex looming over him. Ursa Major quickly lunged forward and sank his teeth into Atomic Rex's powerful arm. The move had hurt Atomic Rex but it also left Ursa Major defenseless.

Atomic Rex opened his huge jaws, and then bit into the bear's shoulders and back. Atomic Rex shook Ursa Major from side to side forcing the bear to release his grip. Once Ursa Major was free of his arm Atomic Rex threw the mutant to the ground. The bear was lying on its side and facing Atomic Rex when the mutated dinosaur kicked the bear in the chest. The force of Atomic Rex's kick drove the thick claws on his toes into the bear's ribcage. Ursa Major roared in anguish as Atomic Rex placed his other foot onto the bear's side and pushed down pinning the animal to the ground. Atomic Rex then opened his jaws wide, reached down, and tore a mouthful of flesh out of Ursa Major's side. Ursa Major continued to struggle and roar in vain as Atomic Rex swallowed most of the flesh on its right side. Ursa Major was still alive as Atomic Rex tore the flesh from his leg and swallowed that as well. Ursa Major struggled for a few more brief moments before it finally bled to death. With Ursa Major no longer struggling, Atomic Rex stepped off the mutant bear and pulled his clawed foot from its ribcage. The kaiju then proceed to devour the remains of his vanquished opponent.

Kate turned her head from the horrifying sight and buried it in Chris's, shoulder. "During my time as Ogre's captive I saw him engage in several brutal fights, but I never saw him eat a creature while it was still alive." Chris quietly hugged her as he continued to stare at the most powerful monster on the planet.

After Atomic Rex had devoured most of Ursa Major, the kaiju walked over to the nuclear reactor silos. Atomic Rex pressed his body against the outside of the reactor.

Chris watched as the monster's body began to glow a bright blue. He whispered to Kate, "He is soaking up the radiation from the reactor right through the wall. He doesn't need direct access to absorb the radiation." Chris made a note in Steel Samurai's logs of the previously unknown method through which Atomic Rex recharged his nuclear powers.

When the kaiju was finished he turned away from the reactor and began heading in a southward direction.

Chris cursed, "Dammit, he is heading in the wrong direction." He turned to Kate. "Climb into my bed and stay there. It's one of the safest places in the mech, and it will keep you from tumbling all over the cockpit. We are going to have to engage Atomic Rex, and I need to know that you are as safe as possible if I am going to focus on what I am doing when I am battling that monster."

Kate grabbed Chris and kissed him passionately before sprinting off to the bedroom. Chris gave her thirty seconds to reach the bedroom and then armed Steel Samurai's high powered guns and missiles. He clenched his teeth, and then he sent Steel Samurai flying directly at Atomic Rex as the mech unloaded all of the firepower at its disposal on the kaiju.

CHAPTER 19

It had been many years since Atomic Rex had felt the sting of bullets and rockets exploding on his body, but the kaiju knew exactly where the projectiles were coming from. The smoke was just starting to clear from around his eyes when Atomic Rex saw the metal giant flying directly at him. Atomic Rex reached into his body to call up a small portion of the nuclear energy that he had just absorbed. The mech was directly overhead when a bright blue dome of nuclear energy emanated from Atomic Rex's body in the form of his Atomic Wave.

Chris saw Atomic Rex's body glowing brighter just before he had reached the kaiju. It had been a long time since Chris had last battled Atomic Rex, and he had forgotten how quickly the kaiju could unleash his Atomic Wave. Steel Samurai had just flown past Atomic Rex when the Atomic Wave slammed into the mech. Chris was thrown about in his chair, and alarms buzzed all throughout Steel Samurai indicating that the mech had suffered significant damage.

Steel Samurai quickly lost altitude and splashed down into the Hudson River. Chris was hanging upside down when his mind cleared enough to check the damage report. There were multiple cracks around the outer hull of the robot that would only get worse with time, but for the moment, the damage was relatively minimal. Chris was lucky that Steel Samurai was already traveling in the direction that the blast had thrown him. Steel Samurai's momentum had allowed him to ride the blast instead of being obliterated by it.

Chris had Steel Samurai climb onto its knees so that its head was just above the waterline. Chris looked out of Steel Samurai's eyes to see Atomic Rex running along the shoreline directly at him. Chris knew that he didn't have time to run so he reacted on instinct and fought. He kept Steel Samurai low in the water until Atomic Rex had nearly reached the robot.

When Atomic Rex stepped into the water and roared, Steel Samurai shot out of the river and connected with an uppercut that snapped the kaiju's jaw shut. Chris followed with three alternating hooks to Atomic Rex's jaw and ribs. The blows rocked Atomic Rex causing him to stagger backward.

Chris had become too engaged in the battle and he forgot the scope of the mission. Rather than focusing on Atomic Rex killing Dimetrasaurs, Chris was thinking about how the kaiju had killed his friends. Chris had the robot deliver two stiff jabs directly into the kaiju's snout, but as he went for a third, Atomic Rex's jaws snapped shut on Steel Samurai's left hand and crushed it like an empty soda can.

Chris finally came back to his senses when he realized that Steel Samurai had already taken heavy damage and that he still had five of the True Kaiju to lure into fighting each other. Chris had Steel Samurai pull its arm out of the monster's mouth, leaving the hand for Atomic Rex to chew on. Chris quickly had Steel Samurai deliver a chop to the base of Atomic Rex's skull while simultaneously sweeping the monster's leg. The end result of the maneuver was that Atomic Rex fell face first into the river.

Chris shot Steel Samurai into the air, and he made sure that he was well out of the range of the kaiju's Atomic Wave before he turned around. He watched as Atomic Rex lifted himself out of the water, and when he did so, Chris fired another volley from his high powered machine guns at the monster. The bullets bounced off of Atomic Rex, who roared, climbed out of the river, and started running along the river bank. Chris was astounded at the kaiju's speed. The beast was charging him at a speed of well over one hundred kilometers per hour.

Chris set a course for Lake Eerie, and then he increased Steel Samurai's velocity to a speed that would keep the robot at safe distance from Atomic Rex.

With Atomic Rex following him into Dimetrasaurs's territory, Chris decided that he needed to see how extensive the damage from the battle was. The first thing that he did was use the internal radio to call Kate. "Kate, are you okay down there?"

Kate's voice came back through the radio, "I got tossed around a bit, but I am good. How are you and Steel Samurai holding up?"

Chris quickly checked on the damage to the mech, with his onboard computer. "There are multiple cracks to the hull, but we should be okay for a good while before they become a problem. We have also lost the mech's left hand."

Kate hesitated a moment before replying. "Is Steel Samurai still functional enough to draw the rest of the kaiju into fighting each other?"

Chris took a deep breath. "I think so, but I am not sure." Chris flew high over Lake Eerie, and then he turned to see Atomic Rex standing at the shoreline and roaring at Steel Samurai. The kaiju then slid into the lake and started swimming toward the mech. Steel Samurai was too high for Atomic Rex to reach him, but Chris wanted to make sure that Atomic Rex was well into Dimetrasaurs's territory.

He shifted the controls forward and Steel Samurai began to drift to the middle of the lake. Atomic Rex followed the mech into the water, and once Chris was satisfied that Atomic Rex would be staying in the lake, he sent Steel Samurai rocketing toward the lake's western shoreline.

When he reached land he headed north and had Steel Samurai submerge itself in the cold waters of Lake Huron. Chris had the mech in water that was just deep enough to cover the robot's head. With the cracks to the outer hull from his battle with Atomic Rex, Chris could not risk subjecting Steel Samurai to excessive water pressure that could further damage the robot. He turned on the radar and saw a few large shapes that were probably mutated fish but nothing that was large enough to be Dimetrasaurs. He set the proximity alarms so that if anything large enough to damage the mech was approaching he would have plenty of warning.

Chris walked down the short flight of stairs to his bedroom where he found Kate sitting on the bed. He stared at her with a defeated look on his face. "I failed. I nearly cost us our entire mission."

Kate reached out for him. "What do you mean that you failed? You got Atomic Rex to follow us into Dimetrasaurs's territory. You were a total success."

Chris shook his head. "Steel Samurai is damaged and was almost destroyed because I wanted to hurt Atomic Rex." His shoulders and his head both slumped. "You were nearly killed because I had a personal vendetta against a monster that killed my two friends." Chris walked over to the bed and sat down next to Kate. "I have to be better than that. I can't let my feelings come before my mission. Steel Samurai is the last hope that humanity has of surviving this hell we live in, and he is my responsibility. I have to be like a stone. I have to block out my emotions and focus on carrying out the mission."

Kate put her arm around him. "You're right in that you are engaged in a mission to save humanity, and the best way to do that is by being a human. I know what's it's like to see a monster kill your friends. I know how the desire to hurt that monster back burns inside of you. If I had a giant mech at my command and I was face to face with Ogre, then I would try to kill him too." She took his hand and kissed it. "It's those emotions that make you human that gave you the strength to move away from Atomic Rex and draw him here. It was those same emotions that caused you to stop attacking Ogre and to save me." She looked into his eyes. "Don't lose sight of your mission, but also don't think that acting like a human will prevent you from accomplishing it either. It's not *Steel Samurai* that is humanity's last hope, it's you. The mech is just the tool that you are using to do it." Kate leaned into Chris's ear, and said, "I guess what I am trying to say is, *trust your feelings, Luke.*"

Chris laughed and so did Kate. She then kissed him on the lips and pushed him back down onto his bed.

On the banks of the Hudson River, Ogre was walking around the remains of the dead giant bear. He sniffed the corpse and once more he smelled the scent of the powerful monster. He also smelled the metal giant, a human man, and most importantly, his pet.

Ogre was extremely hungry from having traveled as far and as hard as he had. The monster took advantage of the opportunity before him and gorged himself on the remains of Ursa Major. Once he was finished eating, Ogre looked into the direction of the Great Lakes, and once more, sprang into the air. Ogre's primitive mind was focused on two thoughts. He had to find the metal giant and the powerful monster. Finding them would lead him to his pet. He would destroy the metal giant and the powerful monster. Then he would claim his pet and return home. As Ogre was at the apex of his leap, he could see Lake Eerie in the distance.

CHAPTER 20

Lake Huron

Chris woke to find that he was still holding Kate in his arms. He was content to just lie in bed with her, until he heard the proximity alarm sound.

Kate woke when Chris sprang out of bed and ran up the stairs to the cockpit.

A moment later and Kate was standing behind him. He was looking out of Steel Samurai's eyes to see a large mutated fish swimming peacefully in front of the mech. Chris let out a sigh of relief. "That mutant is big but it's harmless. Just by looking at the creature's mouth it's obvious that it's a bottom feeder. It doesn't even have any teeth."

Kate smiled. "What's the next step in getting Dimetrasaurs to battle Atomic Rex?"

Chris shrugged. "If Dimetrasaurs is anything like the other True Kaiju that we have encountered, he should be drawn to Atomic Rex like a magnet. Our best bet is to head back to Lake Eerie and see if those two mutated dinosaurs met and battled last night while we slept. I doubt that we would be so lucky. We will probably find Atomic Rex and have to fire a few potshots at him to lure him into following us deeper into Dimetrasaurs's territory. Sooner or later Dimetrasaurs will realize that Atomic Rex is stomping around in his yard, and he will come out to defend his territory."

Chris had Steel Samurai walk to shore where he and Kate saw dozens of giant seagulls roaming about the beach and scavenging for anything they could swallow. Kate was disgusted by the massive birds. "I used to live down by the Sea of Cortez, and I have always hated seagulls. They are not afraid of humans and will eat literally anything. It's no wonder that they have all grown to such gigantic proportions. They probably ate every mutated fish or snail that lived in the lakes."

Chris shifted the controls, causing Steel Samurai to lumber forward. Several of the giant seagulls walked away or took off into the air only to land in the water and bob up and down with the tide. Chris looked at his radar readings. "I'll be glad to get away from these stupid birds. At least then we will be able to see Atomic Rex on the radar. With all of these giant seagulls around it is causing the radar readings to go crazy."

Chris ignited Steel Samurai's thrusters, and the mech flew up into the sky sending even more of the mindless seagulls into the air only to land in the lake.

Several of the seagulls were resting on the waters when a hundred meters behind them a set of twin fins pierced the surface of the water. Like two wide shark fins, the fins darted toward the unsuspecting birds. The bird that was farthest out from the beach was the unlucky creature who meet its doom as the saurian head of Dimetrasaurs came out of the lake from behind it and bit into its back. The rest of the mutant seagulls that had been resting both on the lake and on the beach took to the sky and flew away.

The bird that Dimetrasaurs had sunk its teeth into tried to take flight as well, but the kaiju's grip was too strong for the bird to break. In a vain attempt to defend itself, the giant seagull turned around and began pecking at Dimetrasaurs's head. The bird's beak bounced harmlessly off of the kaiju's thick scales. Dimetrasaurs bit deeper into the bird's back until his fangs sank into the spine of his prey. With his grip secure, Dimetrasaurs began forcing the doomed bird to shore. The giant seagull continued to struggle when it hit the beach, but with one swipe of his claw, Dimetrasaurs ripped the seagull's right wing to shreds. With his prey no longer able to escape, Dimetrasaurs moved toward the seagull's throat in preparation for delivering the death blow. Dimetrasaurs's jaws were reaching toward the seagull's throat and the bird made one last attempt to fight off the mutated dinosaur with his beak. Once more the bird's beak was ineffective as it glanced off of the skull of Dimetrasaurs. Dimetrasaurs clamped his jaws down on the throat of the giant seagull, and with one shake, he snapped the bird's the neck.

Dimetrasaurs then settled down next to the deceased mutant and began feeding on it as he watched the giant mech fly away. The monster had been attacked by one of the giant mechs before, and he was reminded of the attack when he swam by the rusting hulk of the defeated robot when he surveyed his lakes. In addition to the mech, the kaiju could also sense that another of its kind had invaded his territory. Dimetrasaurs was feeding in order to replenish his strength. After the kaiju was done eating, he was going to destroy the robot and slay the kaiju that had dared to enter into his feeding grounds.

Lake Eerie

Atomic Rex was swimming around the western bank of the lake. He had lost the mech that had dared to attack him and now the kaiju was circling the massive lake in an attempt to reacquire his target. Atomic Rex had searched the bottom of the lake thoroughly and taken time to feed off a large fish. The monster had recalled that he has last seen the mech in the sky, and so Atomic Rex swam to the surface of the lake. The kaiju swam slowly along the surface of the water and kept his eyes focused on the sky as he continued to search for Steel Samurai.

Chris was piloting Steel Samurai as the mech soared back toward Lake Eerie. Kate sat on the floor behind him. She was starting to feel somewhat useless. Chris was literally trying to save what was left of the human race, and she was just sitting on the floor. She knew that she was providing Chris with much needed emotional support, but he was also doing the same thing for her. Kate knew that her emotions had been a roller coaster lately. She knew that they had caused her to breakdown in tears a few times, but what human wouldn't be an emotional train wreck in the post-apocalyptic world that they now lived in?

Kate stood. She thought that she might be an emotional mess, just like Chris was, but he was still fighting the good fight, and she needed to do what she could as well. Kate knew that she had her ups and downs but she never saw herself as a damsel in distress. She placed her hand on Chris's shoulder. "I know that the mech is designed to be piloted by one person and that you need to know that I am safe when you are battling a kaiju, but I feel like a burden when I run and hide. Is there anything that I can do to help you out? Even if I am not an active participant in battle there has to be something else I can do while still remaining in relative safety." She walked to side of his pilot's chair so that she could see his face without blocking his view of the sky. "Please give me something to do, let me feel like I am part of your mission and not just a burden."

Chris quickly looked at Kate. The military man in him wanted to reassure her that he had everything under control. He wanted to tell her that she was not a burden, and he was happy to protect her when they were engaged in battle. He wanted to kiss her and tell her that he would make everything better, but as he looked at her, the human being inside of him knew that she needed something else. It was that same feeling of needing to make a difference that drove him to go on this insane mission in the first place. He quickly tried to think of something productive to give her to do that would not take his attention away from piloting the mech.

He smiled at her when he thought of what she could do. "Okay, this may not seem like a big deal, but it's something that will help out in future battles." He brought up a schematic of the interior of Steel Samurai. "We lost the one hand in our last battle with Atomic Rex. I have shut off all functions to that section of Steel Samurai, but the section is still extremely vulnerable to attack." Chris pointed to the repair shop inside of the mech. "Down on level four, inside of the mech's chest, you will find the repair shop. There are blowtorches in there, as well as directions on how to operate them. You will also find long pieces of sheet metal down there and a big magnet to move them with. The sheets are not heavy, and the robot is designed to have the sheets be able to move through it. Use the magnet to pick them up, and then use the blowtorch to weld the sheets onto the wall where the hand used to be. That will reinforce the damaged area. Steel Samurai is designed in sections so that when we lost the hand there is still a wall where the wrist would be, so it's not like you'll be working with open sky in front of you. Still, that section is weak, and a direct hit there right now would take away another chunk of Steel Samurai's arm. Use the steel sheets to reinforce that area. It will help this old robot to hold together while we see this thing through."

Kate smiled, and then bent down and kissed him. "Thank you."

Chris held onto her hand and looked her in the eyes. "Listen to me. The second that you hear me over the radio saying that I am engaging a monster in battle, I want you to shut down the blowtorch and run back to bed. It's still the safest place in the mech, and I won't start an attack until I know that you are there."

Kate smiled. " I promise as soon as I hear you say that you are prepared to engage a kaiju I will shut down and secure the blowtorch and then run to the bedroom."

Chris let her hand go, and Kate then walked out of the cockpit for the first time with a purpose.

She walked down to the repair room where she was easily able to locate a blowtorch and the directions on how to operate it. The blowtorch was a little hand held unit that Kate was confident she could operate without much difficulty. The directions were pretty straightforward and easy for the young woman to comprehend. She grabbed a little carrying case that fit over her back, placed the blowtorch in it, and then slung it over her shoulders.

Finding the sheet metal and the magnet for moving it was also a simple task. The stack of sheet metal was by far the largest thing in the room, and the magnet was resting on the top sheet of the stacked metal. Kate quickly figured out that the magnet had an *on* and *off* switch. Feeling confident that she was finally ready to contribute to the mission, Kate lifted a surprisingly light piece of sheet metal. As she walked to the damaged arm, Kate was surprised at how easy it was to move the awkward sheet metal through the wide hallways and staircases that served as the interior of Steel Samurai. Given all that she and Chris had gone through she had never taken the time to appreciate what a marvel of engineering that the mech truly was. After climbing a few flights of stairs, she found the corridor that would lead to Steel Samurai's damaged arm.

There was a sealed off door leading to the section, and Kate was unsure of how to get to the damaged area until Chris's voice came over the interior radio, "Just hold a second, Kate. I am going to shift Steel Samurai into a vertical position and put its arms down at its sides. That will put gravity on your side. You will be able to drop the sheet metal down the corridor, and then climb down the ladder after it." There was a brief pause. "I have also already checked the integrity of the damaged wrist area. It won't hold up to a kaiju attack but it will more than hold your weight and that of the sheet metal. Just lay the sheet metal over a section of the floor, and then weld it down. I figure that four or five pieces of sheet metal should reinforce the entire wall."

Kate smiled. "Okay, sounds good." Kate held onto the grip next to her as the wall in front of her slowly rotated to the position of being the floor. She took a step back into what was now Steel Samurai's shoulder, and Chris opened the panel. Kate held the sheet metal out over the long corridor, turned the magnet off, and let the sheet metal drop to the floor below her. She then decided that it would be easier to get all of the metal down there before climbing down and starting to weld, so she returned to the repair shop to grab the rest of the sheets required to complete her task.

Chris was flying a canvasing pattern across Lake Eerie in search of Atomic Rex. His plan was to fly across the northern shore of the lake, and then to work his way across the lake in an east west pattern. With each sweep, he would slowly move south until he found Atomic Rex. Chris was looking at his radar when he saw a small target appear on his screen and then fade away. He was unsure of exactly what the target could have been, because it was much too small to have been one of the giant seagulls flying and then diving toward the lake. Chris was ready to forget about the blip until it popped up on the screen again and then disappeared. Chris tried to check the positon of the reading against a topographical map of the area. When he overlaid the topographical map with the radar he realized that the reading was not coming from over the lake but rather along its northern shoreline. The small reading appeared again before quickly disappearing, and it was at the point that he realized what the radar was picking up. Chris whispered to himself, "It's Ogre. Kate was right. That monster has been tracking us this entire time."

Given the damage that Steel Samurai had already suffered, Chris was desperate to avoid a head-on confrontation with the powerful beast. Chris knew that the only way Steel Samurai could be utilized as this point was to get a kaiju to follow it with its long range attacks and then run when he managed to get two different kaiju to engage each other. He thought about alerting Kate to the fact that Ogre was nearby and then he decided against it. She was trying to move past her fear and to be productive in helping to complete the mission. Chris could totally empathize with how she currently felt, and he knew that telling her that Ogre was nearby would only upset and distract her. He also felt that if a confrontation with Ogre, Atomic Rex, or Dimetrasaurs was looming, then he would need the weak section of the mech repaired. Chris opted to change his flight pattern to a north/south direction. He figured that he could cover about half of the lake that way without running into Ogre. He would also keep Steel Samurai over relatively deep water. That way even if Ogre tried to swim out to get him the monster would not be able to leap up to the robot. Chris turned the robot in a southern direction and the blip that represented Ogre quickly disappeared. He was flying south for roughly fifteen minutes when a large target appeared on his screen near the western shoreline of the lake. Since there were no other readings around it, Chris knew that target could not be one of the large seagulls because the ravenous birds always stayed close to each other. Chris was sure that the target most likely represented either Atomic Rex or Dimetrasaurs. He slowed down his pace and then armed the mech's weapon systems.

It took Kate almost an hour but she had finally dropped all five pieces of sheet metal to the bottom of the corridor. Her next move was to climb down the corridor and then stack the sheets into a pile, where she could then grab them one at a time and weld them to the floor. When she reached the floor Kate could feel how cold the wall was that separated her from several thousand meters of nothing but sky. She had been through most of Steel Samurai at this point, and she had never felt the cold from outside. She placed her hand on the floor. "This really is a weak spot in the mech, isn't it." Kate put her gloves and protective face shield on. "Okay then, let's see if we can't add a little more stability to this section." The process of welding was much easier than Kate would have imaged.

She simply laid down a piece of sheet metal and then welded the edges to the floor. She found that it was taking roughly ten minutes to properly weld each piece into place. In less than an hour from when she had started welding, she had reinforced the entire wall. Kate placed her hand on the newly welded sheet metal and was pleased that she could no longer feel the cold air from the outside through the floor. She took a moment to admire her work. "Well Kate, it's not going to win any prizes for looking pretty, but that wall should be much sturdier than it was yesterday."

Kate had just made sure the blowtorch was secure and in the carrying case strapped to her back when Chris's voice came over the radio, "Kate, I have a target that is either Atomic Rex or Dimetrasaurs. What is the status of the repairs to the damaged arm?"

Kate yelled back into the nearest radio, "Repairs are complete!"

Chris's voice came back with a slight touch of surprise in it, "Great job! Now get to the bedroom. I am going to engage the kaiju as soon as I know that you are secure."

Kate immediately starting climbing the ladder to the mech's shoulder, knowing full well that Chris would not want another reply from her until she had made it back to the bedroom.

When she reached the shoulder hallway she sprinted down the stairs that would lead her to the bedroom. She dashed into the room in under two minutes from when she was talking to Chris at the bottom of the Steel Samurai's arm. Kate jumped into the bed and then activated the robot's interior radio. "Chris, I am in the bedroom. You are good to attack."

Chris replied with a quick, "Copy that." He then looked out of Steel Samurai's eyes to see Atomic Rex staring up at him from the surface of the water. As Chris looked into the monster's eyes he almost felt as if Atomic Rex were staring directly at him and not just at the mech. Steel Samurai's chest opened and two sets of missiles armed themselves. Chris pulled the trigger from within the cockpit and the four missiles went rocketing at Atomic Rex. All four missiles hit their target sending an explosion of water and fire into the air that was reminiscent to Chris of his first battle with Atomic Rex back on Coney Island. The kaiju roared but otherwise was unaffected by the attack. Atomic Rex starting swimming toward Steel Samurai, and at that point, Chris started having Steel Samurai drift slowly toward the western shore of Lake Eerie.

Chris watched as Atomic Rex stepped out of the lake, looked up at Steel Samurai, and unleashed an earth shattering roar that was meant to challenge the robot. Chris fired a volley from his high powered machine guns at the kaiju in order to ensure that the beast was sufficiently enraged. Atomic Rex roared once more, and then it began running in the direction of the mech.

Satisfied that he had the kaiju's complete attention, Chris set a course that would lead Atomic Rex along the thick pine forest that served as the border between Michigan and Ontario. He hoped that by staying in the vicinity of three different lakes that he would be able to draw out Dimetrasaurs. Chris kept Steel Samurai heading in a northern direction for roughly twenty minutes until he picked up another radar target. Chris looked at the reading and could immediately tell that whatever was heading for him was very large. Chris secretly prayed the target was Dimetrasaurs. He increased the mech's speed slightly, and within ten minutes, he was able to see two large sets of fins moving across the landscape toward him. A second after the fins came into view Chris was able to see the quadrupedal form of Dimetrasaurs lumbering his way. Chris fired a quick salvo of bullets at Dimetrasaurs causing the monster to roar in anger. Chris then quickly shifted Steel Samurai into reverse so that the robot was backing up toward Atomic Rex.

It took less than a minute of backing up before Chris heard the unmistakable challenge of Atomic Rex from behind him. Chris had the robot fly in an eastern direction so that he was not between the two kaiju. Both Atomic Rex and Dimetrasaurs roared at each other. When neither of the two monsters backed down, the two kaiju charged at each other.

Chris was watching the battle between the two monsters when Steel Samurai was suddenly rocked as if an asteroid had hit. Alarms went off all over the robot, indicating that the outer hull had been damaged near the left shoulder. Chris turned on the exterior camera to see Ogre tearing through Steel Samurai's shoulder as if it were paper.

CHAPTER 21

Chris cursed at himself. With his focus on drawing Atomic Rex and Dimetrasaurs in to a battle with each other, he had neglected to keep an eye on the ever dropping and reappearing radar signature of Ogre, and now the monster was attacking Steel Samurai. Chris quickly turned on the electric field around Steel Samurai. He watched on the camera as Ogre roared in pain but continued to maintain his grip on the outer hull of the mech. Chris realized that he would have to increase the power to the electric field around the robot, but in order to that, he would have to redirect the power from the thrusters that kept Steel Samurai in the sky. In order to save Steel Samurai, Chris would have to land the mech next to the warring Atomic Rex and Dimetrasaurs.

Chris quickly sent Steel Samurai moving backward and down. He landed roughly a kilometer from the kaiju battle taking place before him. He was reaching out to divert power from the thrusters when heard Kate's voice coming over the radio, "Chris, what's happening out there? I thought that we were going to try hit and run against the monsters?"

Chris wanted to lie to Kate. He wanted to keep her from panicking, but he also knew that in order to make sure that she was doing everything that she could do to protect herself she needed to know what was happening. He picked up the radio. "Atomic Rex and Dimetrasaurs are fighting in front of us." Chris took a deep breath. "Kate, listen to me. In addition to Atomic Rex and Dimetrasaurs, Ogre has also attacked us. He is ripping into Steel Samurai's left shoulder. I had to land to the mech in order to increase the power to the electric field and fry that bastard." He tried to sound reassuring, "Kate, don't worry. Just stay where you are, and I will make sure that you are safe. Do you hear me?" The radio was silent as Chis called out to her again, "Kate, do you copy?" Chris decided that he couldn't waste time trying to reach her right this second. He cleared his mind and focused on diverting power to the electric shield.

Atomic Rex sent the pine trees that engulfed his legs flying into the air as he charged the quickly approaching Dimetrasaurs. When he reached the quadruped, Atomic Rex was surprised when Dimetrasaurs lifted himself on his hind legs and wrapped his long front legs across Atomic Rex's neck and shoulders. Dimetrasaurs was much heavier than Atomic Rex, and Dimetrasaurs easily threw his opponent to the ground. Atomic Rex was lying on his side as Dimetrasaurs brought his front legs and the weight of more than half of his body crashing into Atomic Rex's ribcage. Dimetrasaurs's jaws shot out at Atomic Rex's throat, only to be met by Atomic Rex's own jaws. The two monsters bit and clawed at each other until Atomic Rex was able to use his arms to lift Dimetrasaurs off of him.

Dimetrasaurs's legs came crashing down next to his opponent allowing Atomic Rex the chance to scramble back to his feet. Once he was standing upright Atomic Rex darted forward and placed his arms under Dimetrasaurs's body. With one heave, the powerful Atomic Rex flipped Dimetrasaurs onto his side. Atomic Rex lunged at the exposed underbelly of Dimetrasaurs only to be gouged by the monsters flailing claws. The claws of Dimetrasaurs ripped into the face and arms of Atomic Rex causing the mutant theropod to back away. Dimetrasaurs rolled his body back onto his feet, and the two monsters found themselves in the same positions as they were at the inception of the battle.

Dimetrasaurs charged and sank both his teeth and his claws into Atomic Rex's right thigh. Atomic Rex tried to reach down and bite into Dimetrasaurs's neck, but the quadruped continued to shift his body forward causing the razor sharp fins on his back to slice into Atomic Rex's jaw. Dimetrasaurs continued to maul Atomic Rex's leg and to push it backward causing Atomic Rex to fall onto his stomach. The kaiju managed to turn his head to the side in order to avoid being decapitated on Dimetrasaurs's sails, but the sharp protrusions still managed to slice Atomic Rex across his face on the way to the ground.

Dimetrasaurs maintained his grip on Atomic Rex's leg as the kaiju slammed into the ground. Atomic Rex shook his head, and then he saw Dimetrasaurs's short rear leg in front of him. Instinctively Atomic Rex bit into the leg and pulled, yanking

Dimetrasaurs off his thigh. Atomic Rex's thigh was bleeding badly, but he kept his hold Dimetrasaurs's leg. Atomic Rex backed up, dragging Dimetrasaurs with him. Atomic Rex then pulled Dimetrasaurs's leg hard and to the left. The maneuver sent Dimetrasaurs spinning across the forest. Trees were sent flying in all directions as Dimetrasaurs dug his claws into the ground and brought his body to a stop. Dimetrasaurs was facing away from Atomic Rex with his tail swaying back and forth in front of the theropod. Atomic Rex sprinted forward and bit down into Dimetrasaurs's tail. He then secured his grip by digging his claws into the thick midsection of Dimetrasaurs's tail.

Dimetrasaurs roared in pain and tried to pull away, but once the kaiju realized that he would lose his tail before breaking Atomic Rex's grip, the monster changed tactics. Dimetrasaurs bent down with his front legs bringing his head and chest to the ground. The kaiju then pushed hard against the ground and sent his body flying backward with his deadly sails aimed directly at Atomic Rex. In the blink of an eye, Atomic Rex released his grip and saved his arms from being severed off his body, but the sails still impaled themselves deep into the kaiju's chest and shoulders. The momentum of the attack caused Atomic Rex to fall onto his back. The intelligent kaiju rolled with the attack and used Dimetrasaurs's own momentum to roll the monster off his chest. The badly bleeding Atomic Rex staggered to his feet as Dimetrasaurs's rolled over twice before he was able to stop himself and regain his footing. Dimetrasaurs shook his head to clear it, and then he turned his attention to Atomic Rex. When he saw his opponent dripping with blood from his thigh, chest, shoulders, and jaw, Dimetrasaurs roared and the moved in for the kill.

When Kate had heard that Ogre was attacking them it wasn't fear that ran through her mind; it was anger. Kate no longer feared what Ogre would do to her, but she was angry at the thought of the monster hurting Chris or hampering their mission. Kate was running through Steel Samurai to the area that Ogre was attacking. She was determined that one way or the other this would be the last time that Ogre would plague her existence.

Kate had made it to the stairs when the entire interior of Steel Samurai shook like it was standing at the epicenter of an earthquake. The impact caused Kate to lose her footing and slip down several stairs. She had no sooner steadied herself than the hallway shook again. This time Kate was able to grab the handrail that ran along side of the wall. Slowly, she began to pull herself up the stairway and closer to the area that Ogre was attacking. After what seemed like an eternity, she had made her way to the spot where Ogre was pounding away on the outer hull of the mech. The sound in hallway was deafening. It was as if Kate was standing next to a steel smith while he tried to forge a car out of block of iron. She tried to focus on the wall where the sound was coming from, and once she had pinpointed it, she started walking toward it.

In the cockpit of Steel Samurai, Chris watched in disbelief as Ogre continued to pound on the hull of the robot despite the millions of additional volts of electricity that was surging into his body. Chris was trying to have Steel Samurai reach up and pull the monster from of its shoulder, but with Ogre's position and the robot's missing hand, there was nothing that Chris could do. He nearly panicked when he saw Ogre punch the hull with such force that his arm penetrated Steel Samurai. Chris turned around and grabbed a high powered rifle from off the wall behind him. Chris knew that if that monster got inside of the mech that he would head straight for Kate and he would die before he let Ogre get to her. Chris chambered a round in his rifle, and then he quickly switched the view on his screen to the internal hallway that Ogre had just punched a hole into. That was when he saw Kate walking toward Ogre's fist.

Kate was walking toward the sound of the pounding when she saw Ogre's huge black fist smash through the wall. It hung there for a moment, and Kate could hear, see, and smell the incredible amount of electricity that was coursing through Ogre's body as he tried to make his way into the mech. The monster's hand was slowly being pulled back out of the opening it had created, and Kate took the opportunity to sprint down the hallway.

As she was running, Kate pulled the blowtorch from her backpack and lit it. Ogre's face filled the opening that he had created, and when he saw Kate in the hallway, he roared in anger at her. Kate was briefly reminded of the scene in the original King Kong where Kong scaled Ann Darrow's apartment and then looked at her through the window before grabbing her. Kate screamed aloud, "I am no Ann Darrow, and you sure as hell are no Kong!" Ogre was still roaring, and Kate could see the monster's long fangs directly on the other side of the opening. She reached out with her blowtorch, being careful not to touch the electrified sides of the hull, and jammed the burning tool directly into the spot where Ogre's fang connected with his gums. The monster howled in pain, released his grip on the side of Steel Samurai, and fell to the ground below.

Chris watched on the screen in disbelief as Kate managed to fight off the monster that had haunted her for so long. He turned on the interior radio. "Way to go, Kate! I love you!" Chris then grabbed a hold of Steel Samurai's controls and turned the robot around so that it was facing Ogre. The horrible monster was still trying to pull the blowtorch out of his gums. Chris had Steel Samurai take a step and then kick Ogre like a child's ball.

Ogre was flying out into the distance as Kate entered the cockpit. She wrapped her arms around Chris and kissed his cheek. "I love you too." She then looked out the window to see Ogre leaping back toward Steel Samurai. "If we survive this I am going to weld myself a chair in here and hook up a restraint system. No more hiding in the bedroom for me."

Chris nodded and handed her the rifle. "Agreed, for now, I need you to take this rifle. I am going to try and keep Ogre off us but if he breaches the hull again I need you to unload that thing right into his face." He quickly showed her how to chamber a round and fire the weapon. He looked at her. "Are you good to use that thing?"

She nodded in reply.

Chris smiled, "Okay then, head to center of the robot. I will call you over the radio if Ogre latches onto the side again so that you can run there before he manages to tear through the hull." He quickly kissed her, and said, "Just be careful."

Kate nodded and then sprinted off to the center of Steel Samurai.

Dimetrasaurs charged Atomic Rex again, and once more when he was within reach of the kaiju, he reared up on his hind legs. Atomic Rex had learned from the last time that they had grappled that Dimetrasaurs was heavier than he was, so instead of trying to overpower him, Atomic Rex once more utilized a leverage maneuver to neutralize his enemy's attack. Atomic Rex wrapped his arms around Dimetrasaurs, but this time he shifted his legs to the left and pushed Dimetrasaurs to the ground. Dimetrasaurs was thrown to his side again, and the monster started flailing his legs in an attempt to fight off Atomic Rex' jaws only to be struck in the face by the kaiju's thick tail. Dimetrasaurs's head was rocked, and before he could recover, Atomic Rex used his tail to strike him in the face a second time. With his opponent stunned, Atomic Rex realized that his enemy's greatest weapon was also his greatest weakness.

Dimetrasaurs was still lying on his side with his sails perpendicular to the ground. Atomic Rex leaped over the kaiju and landed directly on the flat side of the monster's sails. Dimetrasaurs's body was tilted toward Atomic Rex, and the monster was now helpless to fight off the theropod. Atomic Rex reached down and closed his jaws on Dimetrasaurs's neck, and then he felt the satisfying taste of blood fill his mouth. Atomic Rex shook Dimetrasaurs's neck until he felt the kaiju's neck snap. With his opponent defeated, Atomic Rex looked to heavens and roared triumphantly. He then looked to his left to see the mech that had attacked him several times over the past two days. Atomic Rex roared once again then started walking toward Steel Samurai.

Chris had Steel Samurai pull his sword from the compartment within its leg. He was determined to keep Ogre off of the robot as long as possible. Ogre was in mid–leap when Steel Samurai swung its sword at him. The bladed connected with the monster and sent Ogre crashing into the ground. The monster immediately stood and leapt back at Steel Samurai. Chris used the sword to swat Ogre once again, but as before, other than being knocked off course, the beast was unaffected by the attack.

Chris heard a roar behind him and turned on the rear camera to see Atomic Rex moving away from the deceased Dimetrasaurs and directly for him. He also saw Ogre preparing to leap at Steel Samurai again. Chris turned on the interior radio and shouted, "Kate, throw yourself flat on the floor and hold onto something if you can!" Chris looked out to see Ogre start his leap, and at that exact moment, Chris had Steel Samurai fall to his hands and knees.

As Steel Samurai hit the ground Ogre sailed over the mech and slammed into the face of Atomic Rex. Ogre's blow was so powerful that even Atomic Rex was staggered backward. Ogre fell to the ground where he was standing directly behind Steel Samurai.

Chris shifted Steel Samurai to a position where he was lying flat on his stomach. Chris then turned the mech's boosters up to full speed, and the flames from the exhaust covered Ogre as Steel Samurai skidded through the dense forest. Chris pulled up hard on the controls, and Steel Samurai rose into the air. When he had leveled out Chris quickly called Kate over the radio, "Kate, are you okay?"

She replied, "A few bumps and bruises and I will never eat again before you do that, but I am good."

A wave a relief rushed over Chris at hearing her voice. "Good. We are at a safe altitude now. Get up here. I think that you are going to want to see this."

Kate ran up to the cockpit and looked out of Steel Samurai's eyes to see the smoke clearing around Ogre. Ogre looked around him to see the gigantic foot of Atomic Rex come crashing down next to him. Atomic Rex leaned down and roared at the relatively diminutive Ogre.

Kate sneered at her former captor, "That's right, Ogre. It's time for you to die."

CHAPTER 22

Ogre stared at the massive and enraged form of the blood covered Atomic Rex. He then roared back at the massive creature, leapt into the air, and delivered a punch to Atomic Rex's jaw. The blow shook Atomic' Rex's entire skull. Ogre dropped to the ground, and then he immediately threw his body into Atomic Rex's underbelly.

Atomic Rex staggered backward as the air was forced out of his lungs. The mutant dinosaur was gasping to regain his breath as Ogre leapt onto his back and started to pound on the hard caprice that covered Atomic Rex's spine. Each blow Ogre delivered to the kaiju caused Atomic Rex's entire body to shudder.

Ogre lifted both of his hands over his head, and when he brought them crashing down onto Atomic Rex, the monster fell to one knee.

Kate was watching the battle in disbelief from the cockpit of Steel Samurai. "I don't believe it. Ogre is going to beat Atomic Rex to death. There truly is nothing that can stop that beast."

Chris reached out and grabbed her hand. "I have seen Atomic Rex in action before. Trust me, he is far from defeated. In fact, I think he is about to turn the tides of the battle right now."

Chris directed Kate's gaze back to Atomic Rex, and she saw a blue aura beginning to form around the monster.

Atomic Rex was surprised by the strength and speed of the tiny creature. Atomic Rex had thought that he would crush Ogre, but now he realized that the smaller beast was nearly equal to him in strength. Ogre had managed to position himself out of the kaiju's reach and was pounding Atomic Rex to death. The mutant dinosaur realized that he needed to remove Ogre from his body, and in order to do so, he reached deep into the power contained within his cells. The nuclear energy stored within Atomic Rex's body began to gather just under the kaiju's scales.

Ogre was preparing to deliver another blow to Atomic Rex's back when he began to feel a searing heat burning into his feet. He looked down to see a bright blue light swirling just under Atomic Rex's scales. A moment later Ogre was sent flying into the air as the blue dome of energy that was known as the Atomic Wave dislodged him from Atomic Rex's back. The dome continued to expand as it knocked down every tree in a three kilometer radius from where Atomic Rex stood.

Kate gasped at the sight of the kaiju's Atomic Wave attack. "My God, it was like a miniature atomic bomb just erupted from within him."

Chris nodded. "Trust me, when it hits you that is exactly what it feels like." Both Chris and Kate were suddenly silent when they saw the dark form of Ogre free falling back to Earth.

Ogre slammed into the ground near Atomic Rex. Ogre's impact had created a large depression that he now found himself in. The disoriented monster's entire body was racked with pain due to the fact that his entire top layer of skin had been burned off his body. The monster rolled over onto his back, and he was looking at the blue sky above him when a massive green clawed foot suddenly came into view.

Atomic Rex roared and then brought his foot crashing down onto Ogre. Ogre instinctively threw his hands and feet up in front of himself, and his incredible strength allowed him to stop Atomic Rex's foot from touching the ground. Despite the massive weight that was pressing down on him, Ogre was able to shift his body and to get his feet under himself. The ground beneath Ogre began to crack and split. Ogre's feet were forced into the ground, but still the monster kept Atomic Rex's foot from touching the ground. A second later Ogre heaved upward and he sent Atomic Rex's foot flying back out of the depression. Atomic Rex's foot landed on the ground outside of the impact crater but the move had caused him to lose his balance and to fall flat on his back.

With renewed vigor, Ogre leapt out of the impact crater and onto the fallen form of Atomic Rex. The monster connected with a powerful blow to the ribcage of Atomic Rex.

The theropod roared, and then used his claw to swipe Ogre off him.

The blow sent Ogre tumbling as he crashed through the pine trees of the forest. Ogre crashed through nearly a kilometer's worth of trees before he finally came to a stop. The dark beast sat up to see the colossal form of Atomic Rex walking toward him. Ogre grabbed a large pine tree and ripped it out of the ground. He then turned to Atomic Rex and threw the tree like a javelin at the approaching kaiju.

The tree glanced off of Atomic Rex's snout, but the projectile did little more than to annoy the monster. Atomic Rex roared and then spun around using his large tail like a massive club. The kaiju's tail swept aside dozens of trees before it finally connected with Ogre, and once more, sent the beast tumbling through the forest.

When Ogre stopped tumbling he found himself buried under a small mountain of uprooted pine trees. The beast quickly dug himself out from under the tons of lumber to see Atomic Rex still looming above him. Ogre growled at Atomic Rex, and then he leapt into the air. Ogre's leap had carried him halfway to Atomic Rex when he saw the kaiju's scales begin to emanate a bright blue color. Ogre threw his hands up to shield his eyes, but the rest of his body was hit full force by another Atomic Wave.

Ogre had the sensation of burning and falling at the same time. When his body crashed into the forest Ogre was experiencing a level of pain that he had never felt in his life. Ogre was lying flat on his stomach with his arm in front of his face. Ogre opened his eyes and saw that his right arm was now nothing but exposed muscle and bone. Ogre moaned in pain when he tried to stand. What was left of his tough skin had been burned off, leaving only the muscles below them.

Ogre looked to his left forearm to see that it had burned down to the bone as well. The beast tried to crawl forward, but his body gave out beneath him and he fell back to the ground. Ogre then felt the earth shake beneath him as Atomic Rex walked up behind him. Ogre tried to crawl away again, but Atomic Rex reached down and stuck one of his long claws through Ogre's torso and into the ground beneath it. Ogre writhed in pain as he tried in vain to free himself from the kaiju's claw.

Atomic Rex lifted his claw with the squirming Ogre still impaled on it. The kaiju held the dying Ogre in front of his face and he roared at the monster.

Kate was watching from Steel Samurai, and she screamed at Atomic Rex, "Do it! Kill him! Kill Him!"

As if in response to Kate's request, Atomic Rex brought Ogre to his mouth. One of Atomic Rex's teeth went clear through Ogre's right thigh. Atomic Rex pulled his claw away from his mouth and Ogre let out one agonizing roar as his body was ripped in two. Atomic Rex swallowed the lower half of Ogre's body. Then he yanked the monster's torso off his claw and swallowed that as well.

Atomic Rex looked at Steel Samurai hovering high in the sky above him and as he was staring up at the mech, Kate whispered, "Thank you."

Atomic Rex roared once at the robot, and then he began lumbering over to the remains of Dimetrasaurs. When he reached the corpse of the deceased kaiju, Atomic Rex opened his jaws and tore the dead creature's right hind leg off. He then proceeded to devour his prize.

Chris looked toward Kate. "You're free, Kate. You are finally free. Ogre is gone forever."

She reached down and hugged Chris. "Okay, what's next?"

Chris brought a map of the United States. "Next, we are going to fly back to the East Coast. There may be a few giant mutants but nothing that Steel Samurai can't handle. We are going to land and make some much needed repairs to the robot. From there, we are going to Florida to find the one monster that can match Atomic Rex in terms of raw power."

Kate nodded. "I remember hearing about Tortiraus on the news before Ogre abducted me. Are we going to lure him into a battle with Atomic Rex?"

Chris shook his head. "No. First we are going to lead Tortiraus into Mexico and have him meet up with a particularly large wad of goo. After Tortiraus and Amebos battle to the death, we will have Atomic Rex meet the winner."

Kate kissed him. "It looks like we have a lot of work to do, so let's get moving."

Chris smiled, and then he sent Steel Samurai heading back for the East Coast.

CHAPTER 23

Cape May, New Jersey

Chris and Kate had enjoyed the simple pleasure of sleeping on the beach. It was the first time that they had been able to sleep in relative peace outside since the kaiju had first started arriving. Kate was a little hesitant at first about sleeping outside, but Chris had convinced her that they would be perfectly safe. Chris had landed Steel Samurai flat on its back with the hatch open, and the proximity alarm set. With the alarm set, if anything large did approach them they would hear it and have time to run back into the robot before anything was close enough to attack them. He had also pointed out that Atomic Rex had been going around killing many of the other large and dangerous mutants in the area. After three years of Atomic Rex ruling this area, Chris had figured that most other large mutants had probably learned to stay out of his territory and those that hadn't were probably already killed by the kaiju. Atomic Rex himself was still in Northern Michigan and injured. The kaiju had also recently gained all of the territory from the other kaiju that he had slain, so he would probably take the time to explore his expanded domain.

After hearing Chris's reasons for sleeping on the beach, Kate had finally agreed to do it. The young couple made love on the beach, and after the water had tested clean for radiation, they had even ventured to take a quick swim in the ocean. Given the uncertainty of what could be lurking in the ocean they didn't venture more than few meters away from the shore and safety of Steel Samurai. Still, the cool salt water felt refreshing to the two people who had spent so much time in small and uncomfortable quarters for so many years.

Once their morning swim was complete the two lovers walked back to Steel Samurai. Kate intertwined her fingers with Chris's. "Okay, so what's our next step?"

Chris took a moment, and said, "The first thing that we need to do is use the remaining sheet metal to make repairs to the cracks in

Steel Samurai's hull and to cover the hole that Ogre punched in the robot's shoulder." Chris sighed. "The sheet metal will be little more than a patchwork job. Steel Samurai's exterior integrity will not be nearly as strong as it was before we started this mission. God willing, we will only need to draw monsters into battle with each other two more times. So if we can hold the mech together until then, we will be in pretty good shape."

Chris stood and then started walking around Steel Samurai. He pointed out several large cracks to Kate, "These areas and the hole created by Ogre are our main problems. I was able to take Steel Samurai into the shallow waters just off of the Great Lakes because the water pressure was relatively light. In order to find Tortiraus, we may have to go to the deepest sections of the Gulf of Mexico. If Steel Samurai was in top shape that would not be a problem, but the pressure will cause cracks like these to spread across the mech. This problem is further compounded by the fact that Steel Samurai is faster than all of the kaiju that we have fought so far, mainly because it can fly. When we are underwater, Tortiraus will have a definite advantage over us in speed as well as size, strength, and durability." He looked toward Kate. "One of the reasons that I waited until the last possible moment to engage Tortiraus is because he also represents the kaiju who is most likely to destroy us."

Kate kissed him briefly. "Then I guess that we had better grab the remaining blowtorches and every last piece of sheet metal that we have, then do our best to make sure that this robot can go a few rounds with a giant turtle in his pond." She smiled at him. "I'll work the blowtorch while you carry the sheet metal to all of the different places that we need it. Once you have hauled everything to where we need it, then you can grab another blowtorch and give me a hand."

Chris laughed. "Is that all that I am good for? Manual labor?"

Kate grinned seductively at him. "I can think of a few other things that you are good for, but right now, we have a giant robot to repair." She winked at him. "If you move fast and get this thing done before nightfall maybe I can find time to put some of your other skills to use."

Instead of wasting time replying to her comment Chris quickly climbed back into Steel Samurai, went straight to the repair shop, and grabbed the first piece of sheet metal that he saw.

The two of them worked diligently on making repairs to Steel Samurai, and they had completed their task with several hours of daylight to spare. Kate had even taken the time to weld a chair for herself into the cockpit. She had sanded down the rough edges and used blankets to pad the steel. She had found several straps from some of the extra parachutes in the robot that she was able to use to make a crude harness to secure herself to the chair with. When she was done working on her chair she climbed back outside of the robot to find Chris. She saw him silhouetted against the sun as he was pressing a piece of sheet metal against the side of the robot.

Chris had just finished welding on the last piece of sheet metal when he felt Kate's arm wrap around his midsection. He turned around toward her, and then she pulled him down into the sand where she kept her promise to put his other skills to use.

When they had made their way back into Steel Samurai they both took their chairs in the cockpit. Chris turned the power on, and Kate questioned him, "So off to the Gulf of Mexico, and then to go turtle hunting?"

Chris turned around and smiled at her. "We will probably do that tomorrow. First, we need to make sure that our repairs can withstand a fair amount of water pressure, and we need to replenish some of our supplies."

Chris shifted Steel Samurai forward. The robot strode out into the Atlantic Ocean. As the robot walked through the water both Chris and Kate were able to look out of Steel Samurai's eyes at the ocean around them.

Kate was in awe at everything that she saw. Massive porpoises that had been enlarged by radiation swam by. A giant crab that was curious about the mech walked up to them. It ran its claw over the robot, but once it realized that the robot was not organic, it moved on.

The robot walked for several hours and Chris needed to turn on the exterior lights in order to see in the murky depths. When he turned the lights on Kate gasped at the sight around them. Steel Samurai was surrounded by tens of thousands of tuna. Kate whispered, "My God, those are regular fish. They are not enlarged or anything."

Chris nodded. "We just needed to go out far enough that we were out of the niche that Atomic Rex occupies off the coast. Once we were clear of his regular feeding areas and the Gulf Stream to avoid sea life mutated by Tortiraus, we entered a radiation free area. The fish out here are just *fish*."

Chris had Steel Samurai extend his right arm, and then he pushed a button that caused two large nets to descend from them. A few moments later the net was full of tuna. He then pulled the net back in and the tuna with it.

Kate shook her head. "There must be a ton of tuna in there."

Chris nodded. "Yes, we can only keep a few of them though. I'll end up releasing most of them." He brought up the internal schematics of the robot. "The cargo holds in the floor of the left arm are full of fish. We can open the floor and gaff a few of the tuna. Then we can clean the fish and store them in the refrigeration unit." Chris hit another button. "In the meantime, I am going to have Steel Samurai take on some water. The mech can run it through a desalination process that will make the water good for us to use."

Kate was in awe at the abilities of the amazing machine. She grabbed Chris's hand. "Chris, do realize that if we are able to clear one of the coasts of monsters that you could move the settlement there. With Steel Samurai we could get all of the food and water that we needed from the ocean in order to provide for everyone."

Chris shook his head. "It's not that simple. We can't just clear an area of monsters. Once they kill another monster they take over that monster's territory. Somehow they just seem to know how much land is under their control. With the other monsters gone, and with the exceptions of the South Eastern U.S. and Mexico, Atomic Rex now sees all of North America as his territory. He will take longer loops patrolling his territory, but if there are any humans on what he considers his land he will exterminate them." Chris sighed. "The only way that humans can return to the coasts, or anywhere else but the badlands of the settlement, would be if all of the monsters were gone."

Chris stood. "Come on, let's go clean some fish." He started walking toward Steel Samurai's arm.

Kate whispered to herself, "Is it the land or the resources found there that the kaiju want?"

CHAPTER 24

Atomic Rex chomped down one last bite of Dimetrasaurs, and then the mighty kaiju slumped to the ground. The battles with Dimetrasaurs and Ogre had badly injured and exhausted Atomic Rex. Eating Dimetrasaurs's radioactive carcass would help his incredible healing abilities to start functioning more efficiently, but the kaiju still needed a more direct source of radiation if he was to heal quickly enough to keep himself from slowly bleeding to death. The monster closed his eyes and let his body explore the area around him.

Atomic Rex was taking in all of the information that his body was gathering from the environment. The creature was about to move on from the area when he finally sensed it. There was a large source of radiation nearby. Atomic Rex knew that he would have to force his injured and tired body to walk a great distance and then to swim deep into Lake Michigan as well, but he was left with little choice. Atomic Rex roared to any challenges that might be standing between him and the power that his body craved, and then the kaiju began the long trek toward Lake Michigan.

Atomic Rex was walking across the state of Michigan as blood continued to ooze out of his chest, shoulders, and thigh. The mutated dinosaur moved at a much slower pace than he typically did. Atomic Rex had nearly reached the halfway point of the state when he stopped moving forward. The kaiju sniffed the air and then growled. He could sense a threat nearby. The monster's entire existence was a series of battles for survival and supremacy. Today would be no different.

He looked up and saw roughly ten of the ravenous giant seagulls that patrolled the area flying over him. The birds had sensed the blood that Atomic Rex was losing, and they could tell that the monster was weak and close to death. The birds had been following him from a distance for quite some time, but with each step that Atomic Rex took, the ravenous and single minded birds became bolder. One of the giant seagulls swooped down and missed Atomic Rex's head by only a few meters. The kaiju snapped at the bird as it flew away from him.

The monster took a few more steps before another one of the seagulls swooped down and attacked Atomic Rex's injured thigh. The bird landed next to Atomic Rex and shoved its beak into the kaiju's thigh. The giant seagull grabbed a beak full of flesh and tried to tear it out of Atomic Rex's leg. The kaiju roared, and with one swipe of his powerful claw, he crushed the bird's skull and ended its wretched life. Atomic Rex had killed the first threat to his life, but the nine other birds that were following him had now gone into a feeding frenzy.

The seagulls flew toward Atomic Rex in unison. The giant birds attacked Atomic Rex's already painful wounds. The kaiju felt mouthfuls of flesh being torn from his body. The monster roared in pain, and then he began retaliating against his avian attackers with his claws, teeth, and tail.

Atomic Rex closed his jaws on the head of one seagull and bit it off. He then swung his powerful tail at a bird attacking him from behind. The tail strike hit the bird on the chest, crushed the giant seagull's ribcage, and shattered its heart. Atomic Rex grabbed another seagull in his claws then slammed it repeatedly into the ground, even as the remaining six seagulls continued to feed off of him.

Atomic Rex wanted to unleash his devastating Atomic Wave on the attacking giant seagulls, but he knew that he lacked the power to do so. If he utilized his Atomic Wave then his body would lack the power to continue sustaining him with the wounds that he had recently suffered. The beast was exhausted and his body was racked with pain, but still Atomic Rex refused to yield to his attackers. He swung his tail from side to side, knocking down two more of the seagulls. He slashed his claw at another giant bird and gutted the seagull from its stomach to its neck. He then grabbed another giant bird and threw it into its fellow attacker, knocking both birds to the ground. Atomic Rex stepped on the grounded seagulls, crushing them with his massive weight as he lunged forward and locked his jaws around the wing of the one seagull that was still attacking him from the front.

The bird tried to attack Atomic Rex's face, but the mutated dinosaur shook the bird until its neck snapped. Atomic Rex turned around to see the two seagulls that he had knocked to the ground flying away in retreat. Atomic Rex wanted to roar in triumph at the fleeing birds, but he lacked the strength to do so. The kaiju was covered with blood and feathers. He turned and continued the long walk to Lake Michigan.

For a long hour, Atomic Rex walked under the hot summer sun. Each step that the monster took caused him agonizing pain and threatened to have him collapse from exhaustion, but the monster refused to die. Atomic Rex fought through the pain and fatigue, and finally, he reached the shores of Lake Michigan. He waded out into the water and took a deep breath of air before diving into the lake and letting gravity carry his exhausted body to the murky depths of the lake.

Atomic Rex was fighting to keep his eyes open when he finally saw the rusting form of Metal Master in front of him. The mech had been mostly destroyed in his battle with Dimetrasaurs but its nuclear core was still intact and functioning. There was a deep crack in the mech's hull that allowed some of the radiation from its core to seep out into the lake. Atomic Rex glided next to the mech and rested his body on top of it. As soon as the monster's scales made contact with the mech they started absorbing the radiation stored within it.

As Atomic Rex began absorbing the radiation the awesome properties of his body began to use the energy to heal his wounds. The deep cuts in his chest and thigh were slowly starting to close, and Atomic Rex knew that he would survive. Deep in the depths of Lake Michigan, Atomic Rex growled. The monster's thoughts were focused on the mech that had attacked it twice already. Atomic Rex wanted to destroy the robot, but now he realized that robot could also serve as source of energy for him. Like any prey within his territory he would hunt this mech down, destroy it, and then feed off its energy in the future if he needed to.

The monster's mind began to make other connections as well. It remembered that there were two more mechs like this one back in the city where he had first come to shore. He had not sensed the power within them before because their nuclear cores were heavily shielded inside of the robots. With the mech in the lake, the two in New York, and the one mech that he still needed to hunt down, Atomic Rex would have four new sources of energy for years to come.

When the monster's body had absorbed all of the radiation that it could, Atomic Rex swam back to shore. The monster laid down on the slim shoreline where he would rest and allow his body to heal itself. Once he had fully recovered, Atomic Rex would hunt for the mech that was both a hindrance and a haven to the monster.

CHAPTER 25

The Gulf of Mexico

Steel Samurai stood on the shore looking out over the gulf. This was the most dangerous part of the mission. They would be facing one of two most powerful kaiju in the Western Hemisphere in his own element. The speed and maneuverability that they enjoyed over their previous adversaries was gone. Chris looked at Kate and briefly thought about asking her if she would like him to drop her off at some relatively safe location, but he knew that she would angrily reject the offer. She was as determined to see this quest through as he was. Chris held his hand out to Kate. "Are you ready to do this?"

She intertwined her fingers with his. "I'm as ready as you are. Let's go find that big turtle."

Chris shifted Steel Samurai forward, and the robot started wading out in the blue waters of the Gulf of Mexico. The mech was quickly submerged in the Gulf, and it was at that point, Chris and Kate were able see the effect that Tortiraus had on the ecosystem.

When they were in the Atlantic Ocean, Chris and Kate saw a good number of mutated animals, but Tortiraus had been in the Gulf for almost three years. By this point, nearly everything that lived there had been turned into a colossal monstrosity. Eels as long as buildings swam around Steel Samurai. Fish, each one the size of a city bus, scattered in front of the mech. Shrimp the size of elephants patrolled the sandy bottom of the Gulf. A large shadow passed overhead, and Chris turned on the robot's exterior cameras so that they could see what was above them. The shadow of an alligator that was easily as large as Steel Samurai was floating on the surface of the water.

Chris pointed at the monster. "It must be one of the mutated gators from the time that Tortiraus spent in the Everglades." He then looked at the dozens of readings that were popping up on his radar screen. The pilot shook his head. "The radar is pretty much useless down here. Everything is the size of Tortiraus, so we won't be able to tell his radar signature from all of the other mutants."

Kate turned to Chris. "So how do we find him?"

Chris shrugged. "Tortiraus has never been reported to leave the area around the Gulf of Mexico. Our best option is to work a grid pattern down here until we locate him. Once we do find him we will engage him as quickly as possible, then we will make for the surface and take to the air. From there, we can use our long range weapons to keep him chasing us like we did Atomic Rex when he was in the Great Lakes."

Kate gave Chris a concerned look. "Wasn't there some kind of report about Tortiraus actually flying into the Gulf of Mexico?"

Chris laughed. "Those reports were few and far between. They also came from witnesses who were less than credible. I have seen some strange mutations but there is no way that I can believe that a big turtle has gained the ability to fly."

Steel Samurai worked in a grind pattern walking back and forth across the floor of the Gulf of Mexico for several hours. Over six hours had passed when they finally saw it. It was a colossal shell covered in barnacles and seaweed.

Kate sat down in her chair and secured herself to it. "That has to be Tortiraus, doesn't it?"

Chris nodded. "That's him all right." Chris had Steel Samurai pull its sword from the compartment in its leg. With its sword out in front of it, Steel Samurai slowly crept up to the sleeping kaiju. Chris walked around the massive turtle looking for the opening that held the kaiju's head. He thought that with one well-placed stab that he might actually be able to kill Tortiraus. Then he would only need to draw Atomic Rex into a battle with Amebos, which is something that he would gladly do if Tortiraus was dead.

The kaiju's shell was not like a normal tortoise shell. Chis circled the shell, but from every vantage point, the huge shell looked exactly the same. There were five openings into the shell, only one of which contained Tortiraus's head. Chris had a one in five chance of stabbing the opening which would slay Tortiraus instantly. He looked to Kate. "Any guess which opening that monster's head is hiding in?"

Kate shrugged. "Your guess is as good as mind, but I don't think that continuing to circle him is a good idea. He could wake up any second now. Take your shot now. If you don't kill him at least you will injure him. The other option is to have him wake up and attack us anyway without being injured."

Chris nodded, and said, "I suppose that the opening in front of us is as good as any." Steel Samurai pulled its sword back, thrust it into the opening in front of it, and quickly pulled it out. The sword was covered in blood, and a similarly blood covered claw followed the sword out of the opening.

With speed that no tortoise in the world possessed, Tortiraus's limbs and head emerged from his shell. The furious kaiju stood on two legs and glared at the mech.

Tortiraus roared and moved toward Steel Samurai. Chris tried to back the mech up but underwater the robot walked less than half as fast as it did on land. Tortiraus's raked his claw across the robot's midsection.

Inside the cockpit, Chris screamed, "He breached the hull. I didn't think he could slice through Steel Samurai with one swipe. Water is pouring into the midsection. If I try to take off with the water pouring in it will expand that crack like opening a zipper!" Chris shifted Steel Samurai's controls so that the mech struck Tortiraus across his shell. The blow didn't hurt the kaiju, but it did cause the monster to back up a few steps.

Kate unhooked herself from her harness. "What floor is the breach on?"

"It's on floor twenty-five."

Kate yelled to Chris as she was running out of the cockpit, "Try to hold him off. I am going to try and weld the breach shut!"

Chris took a deep breath. "Hurry up, Kate. I am not sure how long I can keep this monster from hitting us again." Chris shifted his controls once more, and Steel Samurai drug its sword across Tortiraus's midsection. Then the robot followed with a kick to the center of the kaiju's shell backing the monster up even farther.

Kate sprinted down to the repair shop where she quickly grabbed a blowtorch, shoved it into a backpack, and slung it over her shoulders. She then used the magnetic grip to lift a piece of sheet metal, and she ran as quickly as she could to the twenty-fifth floor.

Chris continued to slash at Tortiraus with Steel Samurai's sword. He was only managing to connect with the kaiju's shell, but the strikes served their purpose of preventing Tortiraus from getting close enough to the mech to further breach the hull. Chris was beginning to think that he could hold the monster off long enough for Kate to seal the breach until the monster lifted his legs off of the ground and started swimming around Steel Samurai. Chis was trying to have the mech turn with the kaiju so that its sword was in front of it as a defense. Chris had almost turned one hundred and eighty degrees when Tortiraus swam directly for the mech. The kaiju slammed into the mech and knocked it flat on its back.

Kate had just reached the twenty-fifth floor to see water pouring in through a huge gash in the wall. Kate walked through ankle deep water as she approached the gap. When she made it to the gap, water sprayed over her like a firehose and pushed her away from the wall. Kate threw the sheet metal in front of herself like a shield and began pushing her way to the opening. She had nearly reached the opening when the entire room suddenly started spinning. Between the spinning motion and the water shooting out at her, Kate lost her balance and fell to the floor.

When she hit the floor the water was deep enough to cover her face. Her lungs immediately filled with water and caused her to choke. She sat up and vomited out the salty water. Kate fought her way to her feet and had started to walk toward the breech when the entire room shifted, and once more, threw her to the floor.

Kate was lying on her back as the spray of water increased exponentially. Kate crawled out of the direct path of the water flow and forced herself back onto her feet. Once she was standing she realized the entire room had shifted on her. What had been a breach in the wall had now shifted to a breach in the ceiling. The water pouring into the mech was now being aided by gravity. Instead of standing and wielding a patch to a wall, Kate now had the task of holding a piece of sheet metal over her head and wielding it to the ceiling with the additional force of the Gulf of Mexico pushing against her efforts.

Chris was looking through Steel Samurai's eyes as Tortiraus opened his menacing beak and attempted to tear the mech's head off. Chris had the mech throw its handless arm in front of itself, and the kaiju bit down into the limb. Tortiraus shook his head from side to side, and Chis watched as the majority of Steel Samurai's arm turned to debris right in front of him. He quickly activated the wall that sealed off the section near the mech's shoulder to prevent more water from pouring into the main body of the robot.

Tortiraus was too close to Steel Samurai for Chris to strike the monster with the sword's blade, so Chris used the handle of the sword to hit Tortiraus in the face several times. After the fifth blow, Chris had finally managed to back the kaiju up a few steps. Chris was about to try and get Steel Samurai back onto his feet, but before he could even start the process, Tortiraus was attacking him again. Chris had Steel Samurai drop his sword and use his remaining hand to clamp Tortiraus's jaw shut. He then had the robot wrap his legs around the turtle's shell. Chris knew that the mech could not last much longer in close quarters combat with the kaiju. He whispered, "Come on, Kate. Seal that tear so that we can make a run for it."

Kate positioned herself directly underneath the water pouring down from the ceiling. It took all of her strength to push back against the pressure of the raging water. She pushed the sheet metal over the tear, and her muscles screamed in pain under the strain of holding the sheet in place. Kate tried to ignore the pain and her quickly fatiguing arm. She used here free hand to reach into her backpack and pull out the blowtorch. The slight movement caused the sheet metal to slip out of place, and she had to fight to get it back over the gap. Once the metal was where it needed to be again, Kate quickly ran the blowtorch over a spot in each of the four sides of the metal in order to take some of the pressure off of her arm. With the sheet metal partially welded into place, Kate was able to complete the welding process, and the pouring water was reduced to a drip. Kate waded through hip deep water, and then she hit the radio, and yelled to Chris, "The tear is sealed. Get us in the air!"

Chris heard Kate over the radio and he immediately went into action. Chris had the mech shift its legs against the underbelly of Tortiraus's shell, and he pushed the monster off the robot. He then hit the thrusters on Steel Samurai's feet, and the robot went skidding along the floor of the Gulf. He prayed that Kate was not injured by the sudden movement. Then he had Steel Samurai stand. He looked out of the mech's eyes to see Tortiraus swimming straight for him. He hit the thrusters again, and Steel Samurai began to rise toward the surface. Several seconds later the robot broke the surface of the water and flew into the sky. When the robot was safely in the air Chris called over the radio, "Kate, come in! Kate, are you all right?"

Kate called out behind him, "I am soaking wet and a little banged up, but I will be all right."

Chris turned around and smiled. "Nice work down there. You are becoming pretty handy with that blowtorch."

She slumped down into the chair next to him. "Can we get Tortiraus to swim along the surface and follow us into Amebos's territory now?"

Chris looked below him to see Tortiraus break the surface of the water. "He's below us. I'll fire a few missiles at him to ensure he follows us." Chris armed the mech, and then he fired four missiles at the kaiju. The missiles exploded against Tortiraus's shell, but they did not injure the monster. Chris shifted Steel Samurai forward while keeping his eyes on the kaiju. "It looks like we have his attention .... Oh my God."

Kate ran up to the Chris's seat to see what had caught Chris's attention. Kate looked down through the mech's eyes and gasped when she saw Tortiraus's shell split in two and open up. Beneath Tortiraus's shell there were long wings like those of a beetle. Tortiraus's wings started to vibrate, and the monster rose into the air.

Chris turned to Kate. "Quick, sit down and strap yourself in. We just went from having the monster follow us in the water to having him engaging us in aerial pursuit." As soon as Kate was safely strapped into her chair, Chris sent the damaged mech hurtling through the sky.

Tortiraus roared as the mech flew away from it. The kaiju then rose into the air and flew off in pursuit of Steel Samurai.

CHAPTER 26

Tortiraus was slowly gaining on Steel Samurai as they flew west over the Gulf of Mexico. Kate was looking at the radar, and with each sweep, she could tell that Tortiraus was moving faster than the mech. She questioned Chris, "Can you get the mech to go any faster? That monster is going to catch us before we reach Amebos."

Chris shook his head. "Nearly thirty percent of Steel Samurai is currently held together by patchwork, and we are missing one of our arms. The mech will literally shake apart if I push it much harder than I am now."

Kate saw the blip that represented Tortiraus inch closer to them, "We need to do something, because if Tortiraus catches us in mid-air we are dead anyway."

Chris nodded. "I can use all of our remaining ammunition to target Tortiraus. Losing all of that weight will help to speed us up while also making it easier to maintain the integrity of Steel Samurai. Hitting the monster with everything that we have might even slow him down a little." Chris took a deep breath. "The downside is that if we use up all of our ammunition that we will still have to get either Atomic Rex to chase us down to Mexico to battle Amebos or have Tortiraus chase us across North America to Atomic Rex, without any long range weapons. We will have to engage one of the most powerful monsters in the world in close quarters combat with a mech that's falling to pieces."

Kate shrugged. "Those are both difficult problems to solve, but if we are not alive to solve them, then neither of them will matter."

Chris nodded, and then he began targeting Tortiraus with Steel Samurai's remaining missiles and bullets.

Tortiraus was flying toward the mech when he saw black smoke coming from the robot and dozens of projectiles flying toward him. A second later Tortiraus's body was racked with explosions. The missiles and bullets themselves did not injure the kaiju, but the force of the explosions did slightly slow down the speed at which he flew. The only other effect that the barrage had on the kaiju was to further enrage the creature.

The barrage that Chris had unleashed on Tortiraus lasted for nearly three sustained minutes. When it was over Steel Samurai had lost nearly a ton of extra weight. Chris checked the position on the radar of both the mech and the monster. "We have gained nearly two kilometers on Tortiraus. I figure that we still have about an hour until we reach Amebos."

Kate was almost afraid to ask the question but she forced herself to do it, "Given how fast we are going and the speed at which Tortiraus is chasing us, are we going to reach Amebos before Tortiraus reaches us?"

Chris did some quick calculations. "It looks like we are going to fall about five minutes short and that's *if* Amebos has not moved too far from the area where I last saw him."

Chris grabbed the controls. "Hold on. I am going to try and push Steel Samurai a little harder. It's going to get bumpy in here, and if we start shaking too much I will have to slow down, but I may be able to buy us an extra minute or two. Once Tortiraus gains the extra ground on us I will do my best to out maneuver him until we can reach Amebos."

Kate nodded and grabbed the sides of her chair as tightly as she could.

Chris pushed the thrusters slightly harder, and Steel Samurai began to shake as if it were an old building trying to endure an earthquake. Chris could feel the robot jump forward a little bit—indicating an increase in speed, but when he looked down at his radar he saw the blip that represented Tortiraus moving ever closer to Steel Samurai.

Twenty minutes had passed with Steel Samurai threating to shake apart under the stress that it was enduring while Tortiraus continued to creep ever closer to the once mighty mech.

Kate called out, "Do you have Amebos on radar yet?"

Chris shook his head. "Amebos is not solid enough to give a radar reading. If it is in the middle of absorbing something we might be able to pick it up, but more than likely, we will have to find it visually."

Chris dropped Steel Samurai through the clouds over the area where he had last encountered Amebos. He breathed a sigh of relief when saw that the mountain of goo was still in the same spot that it was when he had led the Colony into Amebos. Amebos had no sooner come into view than Steel Samurai was rocked as Tortiraus latched onto the giant robot.

Tortiraus gouged Steel Samurai across its back with his claws and his beak bit a chunk out of the robot's shoulder. Chis spun Steel Samurai around and had the mech start delivering punches to the kaiju. Chris knew that he was not going to be able to fight Tortiraus off the mech. He could see that the kaiju had already torn open several new gashes in the mech, and this time, sheet metal would not be able to repair the damage. Tortiraus was shaking Steel Samurai from side to side, and Chris quickly realized what his only option was. "Kate, brace yourself. I am going to take us directly into Amebos!"

Chris had Steel Samurai wrap his arm around Tortiraus, and then he flew straight at Amebos. The two grappling giants splashed down in the viscous fluid that was Amebos. Once they were inside of Amebos, Tortiraus began screaming in pain. Chris used the opportunity to push the kaiju off the mech.

One they were free of the kaiju's grip, Chris reactivated the thrusters, and Steel Samurai flew out of Amebos and into the sky. Chris looked down to see the scales melting away from Tortiraus's body as Amebos started to devour the kaiju. He was content to watch Tortiraus be dissolved into nothing until he heard Kate scream. Chris turned around to see a three meter wide piece of Amebos slithering into the cockpit.

Kate immediately unhooked herself from her seat, grabbed the shotgun, and began unloading it at the piece of Amebos. The bullets passed harmlessly through the gelatinous mass as it continued to crawl forward. Kate yelled at Chris, "Is there a fire extinguisher in here?"

Chris had turned his attention to the external cameras where he saw more pieces of Amebos crawling into the other holes that Tortiraus had created on Steel Samurai. He yelled back to Kate, "It's under my seat. Why?"

Kate ran to Chris's seat. "Haven't you ever seen *The Blob*?" Kate grabbed the fire extinguisher and emptied it on the piece of Amebos. The section of Amebos writhed back and forth until it was frozen solid. Chris has seen what Kate did, and yelled, "Get up here next to me. You just gave me an idea about how to get rid of the pieces of Amebos that are still clinging to us, but I only have one oxygen mask. Kate ran up next to Chris and grabbed onto him as Chris pulled an oxygen mask out of his control panel and sent Steel Samurai ascending even higher into the atmosphere.

Tortiraus could feel the scales being burned off his body. He pulled his extremities into his shell but even that offered no protection as the fluid like Amebos was able to make its way through the openings in the kaiju's shell. Tortiraus poked his head back out of his shell, and he started to spew acid from his mouth into Amebos. As the acid came into contact with Amebos's body, the two chemicals began to combined and form a white foam. Tortiraus could feel the pain of Amebos lessening as he continued to spew acid into the formless monster.

Chris and Kate were hugging each other for warmth and passing the oxygen mask back and forth between the two of them as they each struggled to maintain consciousness. The thin air was making it cold and difficult to breath, but it was also slowly freezing the pieces of Amebos that were clinging to Steel Samurai. Chris could see small sections of the pieces crystalizing and breaking off the robot. He tried to tell Kate but the air was too thin for him to talk. He was starting to blackout when Kate put the oxygen mask onto his face. He took a breath and looked down to see Kate passed out on his lap. Chris focused his eyes on the external camera's to see the last pieces of Amebos breaking off in frozen crystals and falling back to Earth.

He turned Steel Samurai around and began descending back to Earth. As the air became thicker Kate slowly started to wake up. When she regained consciousness she looked at Chris and smiled. A few seconds later, they looked through Steel Samurai's eyes to see a mountain of white foam where Amebos had been. Chris stared at the foam. "What happened to Amebos and Tortiraus?"

In answer to part of his question, Tortiraus poked his head out of the foam. The kaiju's face was missing scales, and it was bleeding, but the he was alive.

Kate pointed at the foam. "Tortiraus spews out acid. Amebos must have been composed of mainly a base. Look at the mound of foam. It looks just like those clay volcanoes that we used to make as kids. We would put baking soda in the middle of the volcano and then pour vinegar on top of it. The acid and the base would make a chemical reaction that would leave behind foam that looked exactly like that."

Chris flew over the mound to get a closer look at it. "So is Amebos dead?"

Kate shrugged. "I guess so." Their speculation was cut short when Tortiraus saw Steel Samurai circling overhead. The kaiju roared, crawled out of the foam that had once been Amebos, and spread its wings. Chris could immediately see that the wings had suffered some damage from his battle with Amebos. Chris shouted, "He's hurt! He might not be able to fly as fast as he could before. We might be able to stay ahead of him until we find Atomic Rex. If we travel at Steel Samurai's top sustainable speed we can reach the Great Lakes in just over two hours."

Kate kissed Chris, "All right then, let's end this." She climbed back into her chair, and once she was strapped in, Chris sent Steel Samurai flying north.

Tortiraus roared and took off into the air in pursuit of the mech.

Chris was watching the kaiju on his external camera while also surveying the damage to the mech. Steel Samurai was barely holding together. The damage from attacking the kaiju had left the mech functioning at less than twenty percent of its optimal capacity. He tapped the control panel if front of him. "Come on, *old girl*. You have one more trip left in you."

CHAPTER 27

Atomic Rex stirred on the shores of Lake Michigan. The mighty kaiju opened his eyes and snarled. The monster had many senses that were far beyond the understanding of science. One of those senses was Atomic Rex's ability to detect when another kaiju was nearby. Even more than a just any kaiju, Atomic Rex could sense that it was Tortiraus coming toward him.

Atomic Rex feared no other creature on the planet, but he was aware that Tortiraus was a significant threat to him. The two kaiju had long been aware of each other's existence, and until this point, they had managed to avoid each other. Whatever the reason for Tortiraus's desire to attack him, Atomic Rex was prepared to meet his rival and destroy him.

Atomic Rex could sense that Tortiraus was not far away. The kaiju considered walking out to meet the giant turtle but reconsidered that course of action. He was well aware that a battle with Tortiraus would tax his abilities to their limits. He had an ample supply of food and radiation in the lake. The kaiju decided that it would be best to wait at the lake if Tortiraus was coming to him. When Tortiraus arrived he would slay the beast, then he would feast off of the turtle's remains, and finally he would recharge his radioactive powers from the mech at the bottom of the lake. Atomic Rex turned to his left and the impatient kaiju began to pace back and forth along the southern shore of Lake Michigan.

Kate was reduced to doing little more than sitting next to Chris again, but she was unsure of what exactly she could do at this point to help him out. She could see the intensity in Chris's eyes as he continued to push Steel Samurai toward the last known location of Atomic Rex. She could see that as they neared the improbable completion of their quest that he was also pushing himself as hard as he could to complete it. Kate mused that perhaps simply talking to Chris and serving as sounding board for him may be the most important thing that she could do at this time. She placed her hand on Chris's shoulder. "Are we still staying a safe distance ahead of Tortiraus?"

Chris nodded. "Yes, given our condition this is pretty much Steel Samurai's top speed, but with the damage that Amebos caused to Tortiraus's wings, this seems to be about his top speed too."

Kate leaned in a little closer to her lover. "How far are we from Atomic Rex?"

Chris pointed to a large blip on his radar screen. "That's him. He is just pacing in a small area. He probably can sense that Tortiraus is heading straight for him, and he is waiting to attack. We should be able to see him within the next fifteen minutes." He looked quickly toward Kate. "I have barely escaped two encounters with Atomic Rex when Steel Samurai was functioning at one hundred percent. You realize that there is a very good chance that our luck has finally run out. This may be a *one way trip* for us."

Kate kissed his cheek. "Chris, you have already succeeded in your mission. All of the other True Kaiju are dead, and you have Tortiraus heading directly at Atomic Rex. In the next hour, either one or both of them will be dead. You have given the human race a chance at survival. You are a hero." She turned his head slightly so that he was looking at her. "If this is the end of the road for us then there is nowhere else that I would rather be. Before I met you I didn't think that things like *hope* and *love* still existed in this world, and you have shown me that they do. I can't assure you as to what will happen today, but I can assure you that I love you and that I am proud of you." She kissed him again, and then she sat back in her chair as she waited for the longest fifteen minutes of her life to pass by.

Atomic Rex continued to pace until the odor of Tortiraus finally reached his nostrils. It was the same foul stench that the kaiju had encountered when he had battled Marsh-Thing several days ago. Atomic Rex stared to the south and roared a challenge at the approaching Tortiraus. The kaiju then noticed that an object was coming toward him in the sky. The kaiju had assumed that the form was Tortiraus, but when it came into better view, he saw that it was the mech who had attacked him earlier. The same mech who could provide him with another source of the radiation that his body craved.

The mech streaked directly at Atomic Rex. The monster ran toward the incoming mech, but at the last second, the mech pulled up and flew into the sky. Atomic Rex looked up and roared at the fleeing mech. His head then snapped forward as the massive form of Tortiraus slammed into his body.

The two kaiju tumbled over each other several times before Atomic Rex was finally able to push the gargantuan turtle off him. Anger coursed through Atomic Rex at the sight of his longtime nemesis. The mutated dinosaur unleashed a fury filled roar at the turtle.

Tortiraus pushed his body into a bipedal position, and then he hissed at Atomic Rex. There was no sizing each other up. Both of the kaiju knew exactly how powerful their opponent was. For three long years, their territories had border each other and neither one of the two had dared to challenge the other, but now here they were finally face to face.

Steel Samurai leveled off in the sky above the two kaiju. Chris had the mech remove its sword from the compartment in its leg. Then he stared down at the two monsters, with the intensity of a man obsessed.

Kate grabbed his hand. "What happens now?"

Chris kept his eyes fixed on the kaiju. "Now they battle to the death. Once one of them has killed the other I will have Steel Samurai plunge its sword through the victor, and we bring an end to the age of kaiju!"

Atomic Rex charged Tortiraus, and the theropod slammed into the center of the colossal tortoise. The blow caused Tortiraus to stagger backward, but he managed to maintain his footing. Atomic Rex stepped forward and wrapped his arms around the sides of Tortiraus's shell while simultaneously trying to bite into the turtle's shoulder. Despite his best efforts, Atomic Rex quickly realized that not even his powerful teeth and claws would be able to penetrate the shell of Tortiraus.

Tortiraus raked his right claw across Atomic Rex's snout, drawing blood in the process. He then raked his left claw across the theropod's lower jaw gashing that open as well. Atomic Rex took a step backward, and Tortiraus used the extra space to use his shell like a battering ram to knock Atomic Rex to the ground.

Atomic Rex rolled with the blow and put some distance between himself and Tortiraus before returning to his feet. Tortiraus took a step forward, and as he did so, Atomic Rex spun around and sent his thick tail crashing into Tortiraus's side. While the theropod's tail hit the turtle's shell with enough force to crush the side of a skyscraper, Tortiraus was totally unaffected by the blow.

Tortiraus took another step forward, and then dug his claws into Atomic Rex's side. Tortiraus pulled Atomic Rex to his left, and then he threw him to his right—sending the mutated dinosaur crashing into the ground. Atomic Rex's entire body shook when he hit the ground. The kaiju was lying on the ground momentarily stunned as Tortiraus took a step forward and kicked him in the ribs.

The surging pain brought Atomic Rex back to his senses. The theropod saw Tortiraus's foot in front of him, and he clamped his jaws down on them. Atomic Rex then pulled his jaws back and Tortiraus's foot with them, causing the giant turtle to fall flat onto his back.

The instant that Tortiraus landed on his back the giant turtle instinctively pulled his extremities inside of his shell. Seeing his opponent in what appeared to be a vulnerable position, Atomic Rex jumped on top of Tortiraus's shell, and once more, he began biting and clawing at the thick covering. After a few unsuccessful attempts to penetrate the shell, Atomic Rex realized that even when Tortiraus was down that he would not be able to tear through the turtle's shell. Atomic Rex jumped off of Tortiraus and turned his back to the monster.

Atomic Rex then lifted his tail high into the air and brought it crashing down onto Tortiraus. Atomic Rex had repeated the move several times until Tortiraus's head popped out of his shell, and he used his powerful beak to bite into the dinosaur's tail. Atomic Rex roared in pain as he tried to pull away from the vicious bite, but in doing so, he only managed to pull Tortiraus back onto his stomach.

Tortiraus unsheathed his claws from his shell, and then he pushed himself back to his bipedal position while still holding Atomic Rex's tail in his beak. The move caused Atomic Rex to lose his balance and fall onto his face. Atomic Rex's jaw snapped shut as it crashed into the ground. Atomic Rex was lying on the ground with his tail still trapped in Tortiraus's beak when the huge turtle started to back up. As Tortiraus walked backward, he dragged Atomic Rex along the ground using the very terrain itself to tear at the theropod's chest and stomach.

Atomic Rex was in intense pain as a layer of scales was being shredded off his body. The kaiju was trying to pull free of the turtle's grip when he remembered his battle with Dimetrasaurs. Atomic Rex had Dimetrasaurs in a similar positon, and the monster had managed to break free of the grip in an unorthodox manner. Atomic Rex dug his claws into the ground creating as much resistance as he could to Tortiraus's pulling motion. The moved caused a temporary halt to Tortiraus's momentum. Atomic Rex used the brief stop to push off of the ground as hard as he could—which sent his body flying directly at Tortiraus. Atomic Rex's body hit Tortiraus with the force of a hurricane, causing the turtle to release his grip on the theropod's tail. Tortiraus tumbled to the ground as Atomic Rex sprang to his feet.

Atomic Rex roared at the downed Tortiraus, indicating his desire to end the battle. Atomic Rex's body briefly took on a blue aura, and then the kaiju unleashed the power of his Atomic Wave.

When Tortiraus saw Atomic Rex powering up he pulled himself into his shell. The blue dome of pure radiation swept across the ground and hit Tortiraus's shell throwing the giant turtle into the air. Tortiraus flew through the air for several seconds before he came crashing back down to Earth. Atomic Rex started walking over to his defeated enemy when, to his astonishment, Tortiraus's head, arms, and legs all came out of his shell totally unscathed by the attack. By staying within the protective covering of his shell, Tortiraus had managed to ride out the force of Atomic Rex's attack.

Tortiraus roared as he lunged forward and grabbed Atomic Rex by the arms. With his enemy trapped in his grasp, Tortiraus employed his most powerful weapon. The giant turtle opened his beak and began spewing acid onto Atomic Rex.

Atomic Rex could feel the acid burning through his thick scales and into the muscles below them. The mutated dinosaur roared in pain as he knew that he was dying.

The second that the thought of death crossed Atomic Rex's mind the kaiju forced it out. The beast refused to die, and he refused to be defeated! Atomic Rex dug his claws through Tortiraus's fleshy arms and into the bones within them. Then, despite being dissolved alive by the turtle's acidic spray, Atomic Rex once more called forth the nuclear energy stored within his body.

Tortiraus tried to retreat into his shell again, but Atomic Rex held the monster in place. The Atomic Wave immediately burned away the tissue on Tortiraus's arms, reducing the limbs to nothing but bones. Atomic Rex's grip on Tortiraus also prevented him from riding along the Atomic Wave. As the wave continued to run through Tortiraus, bright blue cracks began to form on the kaiju's shell. Milliseconds after the cracks formed, Tortiraus's entire shell shattered exposing the fragile body contained within it. Tortiraus stopped spewing acid, and a moment later, the mighty kaiju died.

Atomic Rex dropped the charred remains of Tortiraus to the ground and started to unleash a victory roar when Steel Samurai plunged its sword into the kaiju's back and through his chest. Blood spurted from Atomic Rex's mouth as his lungs filled up with the life sustaining fluid.

Chris had Steel Samurai pull the sword from Atomic Rex's back. He then had the mech lift the sword over its head in preparation for decapitating the kaiju. Before the mech could bring the sword down, Atomic Rex slashed his claw across the mech's chest, tearing it open. He then clamped his jaws around Steel Samurai's remaining arm and tore it off. Rather than finishing the mech, the mortally wounded kaiju stumbled into Lake Michigan and disappeared into the water.

Chris cursed, "Dammit! With the damage to the mech, I can't follow him into the water. I can't be sure that he is dead!"

Kate placed her hand on his shoulder. "He had most of the scales burned off his body, and then you skewered him with Steel Samurai's sword. If he is not dead he soon will be." She kissed Chris. "You did it. You saved the world, and you are still alive to celebrate it." She hugged him. "Now, didn't you tell me that there was a settlement of people who you need to check on and spread this good news to?"

Chris nodded. "You are right. Atomic Rex must be dead. And *yes*, there is an entire settlement of people, who if they are still alive, need to know that a world without kaiju is waiting for them.

EPILOGUE

Kansas

The severely damaged form of Steel Samurai slowly flew toward the location of the settlement. As the tent city came into view, Chris gasped when he saw that the entire edge of the settlement had been torn to shreds.

Chris had started to tear up when Kate walked over and hugged him. "It is okay. It looks like only part of the settlement was destroyed. The majority of the tents look unharmed. There is a good chance that most of the people here are still alive."

Chris nodded as he gently landed Steel Samurai on the outskirts of the settlement. Hundreds of people came out of the remaining tents and slowly walked toward Steel Samurai. Chris opened the hatch, and then he and Kate began the long climb down the side of the mech to the ground below.

By the time Chris had reached the ground, nearly a thousand people had surrounded Steel Samurai. At first, the people just stared silently at Chris, and he did the same to them. Kate jumped off the ladder and walked up to Chris and grabbed a hold of his hand.

She had no sooner grabbed his hand than the first shout came from the gathered crowd, "There he is! Thanks for leaving us with no protection, coward. I lost most of family in the last mutant attack."

The first accusation was followed by dozens of more shouts, accusations, and curses. Chris stood there and let the crowd vent their collective anger at him, while Kate continued to hold his hand. Finally, one of the town leaders made his way to the front of the crowd. He stood in front of them and made hand motions for the gathered people to calm down.

Once the crowd had stopped shouting, the elder walked up to Chris. "Captain Myers, to put it bluntly, you are not welcome here. Only two days after you had abandoned us, a giant vulture descended from the sky and devoured the entire northern end of the settlement. Hundreds of our people died. Their deaths fall on your head, Captain Myers!" The leader looked at the remains of Steel Samurai. "I see that you have even managed to destroy the only remaining guardian that we had." The settlement leader took another step closer to Chris. The leader pointed at Chris, and started shouting, "Take a look around you, Captain Myers. You have sentenced all of us to death. You have sentenced the last remnant of the human race to extinction."

Kate had finally had enough. She stepped forward and started shouting at the leader as well as the gathered crowd, "You people have no idea what you are talking about. You should all be thanking him. Because of his actions all, of the True Kaiju are dead!"

A collective gasp echoed through the crowd.

Kate shook her head in affirmation of their surprise. "Tortiraus, Giladon, Ogre, they are all dead. Chris has made it so that you no longer have to be trapped here in the settlement. You can move back to the coasts, back to cities, back to an ample supply of food, water, and tools."

The settlement leader looked at Chris. "Is this true? Are the kaiju dead?"

Chris nodded. "Yes."

The leader glared at Chris again. "What about the giant mutants which still roam the planet? With Steel Samurai in ruins, we have no protection against these lesser monsters."

Kate walked up into the leader's face. "We know that the remains of two other mechs are still at Coney Island. With access to the factories and the resources there, surely we can scavenge enough pieces from those mechs to repair Steel Samurai."

When Chris heard Kate say those words he smiled. He had never thought about using the spare parts from his friend's mechs. In a way, he almost felt as if by using their mechs to repair Steel Samurai that they would still be helping him to defend the remaining humans on Earth.

The settlement leader turned to Chris, with an astonished look on his face. "You have accomplished all of this, Captain Myers?"

Chris looked toward the woman he loved. "None of it would have been possible without Kate."

Kate hugged Chris, and then she shouted to gathered crowd, "People of the settlement, give your thanks to Captain Chris Myers, the slayer of the kaiju."

A cheer ran throughout the crowd, and the settlement leader could see that he was quickly losing control of the crowd to Kate. He stepped forward and proclaimed, "We are all thankful to Captain Myers!" He pointed at Chris and Kate. "I and the other leaders shall work with these two heroes to formulate a plan to move us out of the settlement and back to coasts!"

The crowd cheered, and then the leader led Chris and Kate to his cabin.

Three months later

Due to her charisma and natural leadership abilities, Kate had quickly risen to be one of the leaders of the settlement. She had overseen the plans to relocate the citizens of the settlement. The majority of the people moved to the Pacific Northwest. Due to the fact that Yokozuna was not by nature an aquatic monster, the giant did not spend much time in the ocean, resulting in most of the sea life in the Pacific waters being radiation free. Additionally, the gluttonous giant had devoured most of the creatures that his radiation had created, resulting in there being a relatively low threat of mutant attack. The people who were sent there started building permanent housing and fishing ships.

Chris had led a small group of people to Coney Island where they used several manufacturing plants to take parts from Iron Avenger and Bronze Warrior. When the mech was complete, Chris felt that the composite robot was a fitting tribute to his deceased friends and their memory. Once Steel Samurai 2 was operational Chris took the people who had helped him to the West Coast where the mech was able to assist in fishing and using his internal components as a desalination plant, providing the people with fresh drinking water.

After Chris had returned to the Northwest, he and Kate took the mech to Lake Michigan. They searched the lake both visually and with radar for the remains of Atomic Rex, but they weren't able to find anything. They did, however, find the remains of the Metal

Master rusting at the bottom of the lake. A quick reading from a Giger counter confirmed that the mech was leaking radiation. Chris sighed. "Three months is a long time I suppose that the fish and mutants in the lake could have dispersed the remains of Atomic Rex."

Kate stared at the Giger counter. "There is also the chance that Atomic Rex was able to heal himself from the radiation coming from the mech and that he has been eating the fish in the lake."

Chris looked Kate in the eyes. 'What do you want to do?"

Kate brought up a map of the Great Lakes area. "We still have the nuclear reactors from Iron Avenger and Bronze Warrior, right?" Chris nodded. Kate pointed at various points on the map. "Okay I want to leave their reactors at two points several hundred kilometers from Lake Michigan. I want them to form a huge square with the remains of Metal Master and the nuclear power plant on the Hudson River. I think that if Atomic Rex is still alive and we supply him with enough, land, food, and radiation that he will leave us alone." She turned to Chris. "If he is alive we will effectively be giving him the entire eastern half of the United States."

Chris nodded. "Seems like a good plan to me. Can we go home now?"

Kate gave Chis a sly smile. "Fly us about halfway home and then park the mech. There is something else that I need to address with you before we go home."

Chris smiled at her. "Yes, ma'am." He then activated Steel Samurai 2's thrusters, and the robot flew off into the sky.

THE END

CHECK OUT OTHER GREAT KAIJU NOVELS

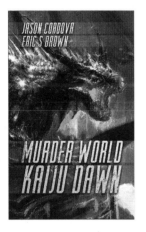

MURDER WORLD | KAIJU DAWN
by Jason Cordova
& Eric S Brown

Captain Vincente Huerta and the crew of the Fancy have
been hired to retrieve a valuable item from a downed
research vessel at the edge of the enemy's space.
It was going to be an easy payday.
But what Captain Huerta and the men, women and alien
under his command didn't know was that they were being
sent to the most dangerous planet in the galaxy.
Something large, ancient and most assuredly evil resides
on the planet of Gorgon IV. Something so terrifying that
man could barely fathom it with his puny mind. Captain
Huerta must use every trick in the book, and possibly write
an entirely new one, if he wants to escape Murder World.

KAIJU ARMAGEDDON
by Eric S. Brown

The attacks began without warning. Civilian and Military
vessels alike simply vanished upon the waves. Crypto-zool-
ogist Jerry Bryson found himself swept up into the chaos
as the world discovered that the legendary beasts known
as Kaiju are very real. Armies of the great beasts arose
from the oceans and burrowed their way free of the Earth
to declare war upon mankind. Now Dr. Bryson may be the
human race's last hope in stopping the Kaiju from bringing
civilization to its knees.
This is not some far distant future. This is not some alien
world. This is the Earth, here and now, as we know it today,
faced with the greatest threat its ever known. The Kaiju
Armageddon has begun.